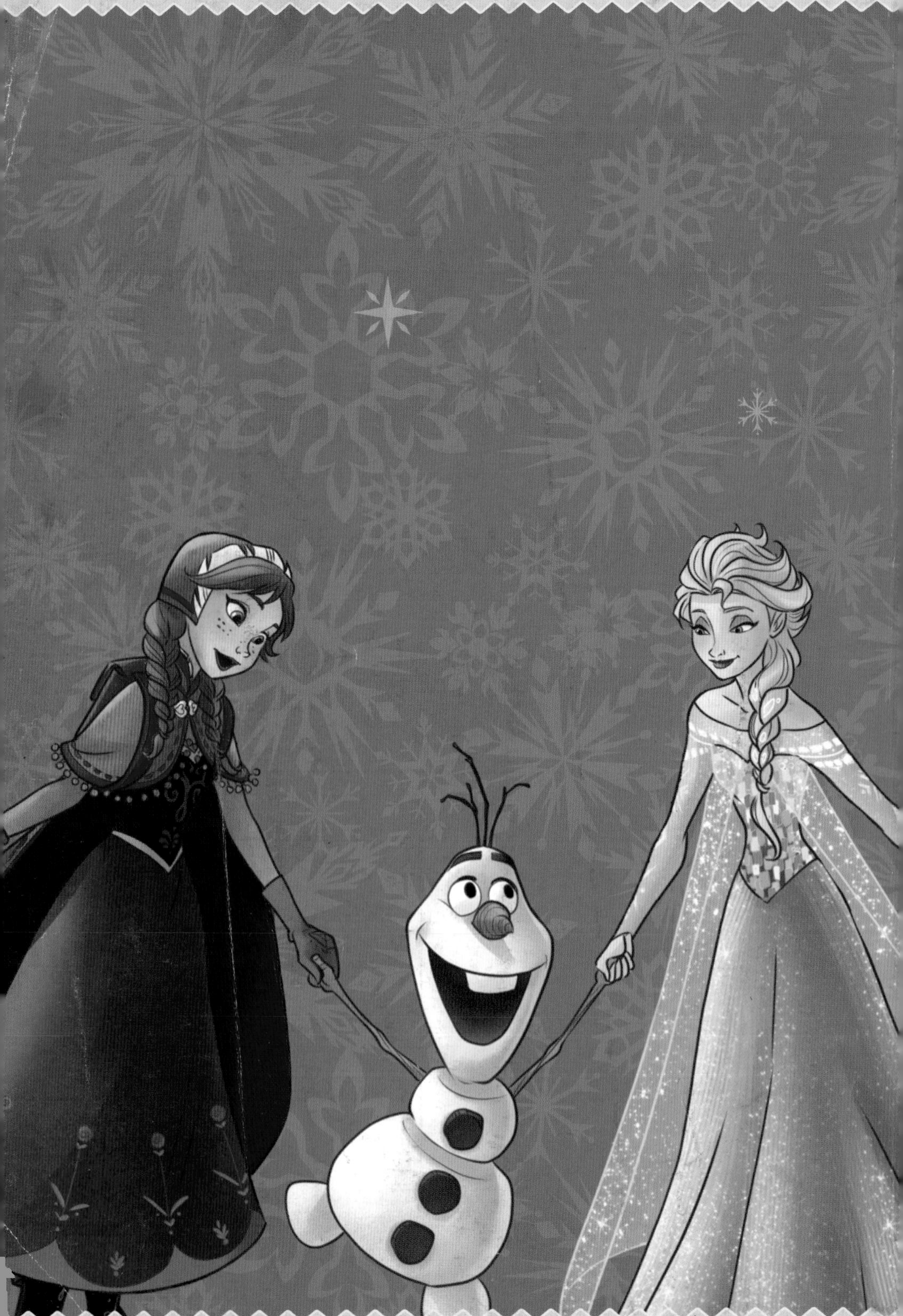

Disney

FROZEN

⟨ ADVENTURES ⟩

SNOWY STORIES

DARK HORSE BOOKS

DARK HORSE BOOKS

PRESIDENT AND PUBLISHER
MIKE RICHARDSON

COLLECTION EDITOR
FREDDYE MILLER

DESIGNER
SKYLER WEISSENFLUH

COLLECTION ASSISTANT EDITOR
JUDY KHUU

DIGITAL ART TECHNICIAN
SAMANTHA HUMMER

Neil Hankerson Executive Vice President **Tom Weddle** Chief Financial Officer **Randy Stradley** Vice President of Publishing **Nick McWhorter** Chief Business Development Officer **Dale LaFountain** Chief Information Officer **Matt Parkinson** Vice President of Marketing **Cara Niece** Vice President of Production and Scheduling **Mark Bernardi** Vice President of Book Trade and Digital Sales **Ken Lizzi** General Counsel **Dave Marshall** Editor in Chief **Davey Estrada** Editorial Director **Chris Warner** Senior Books Editor **Cary Grazzini** Director of Specialty Projects **Lia Ribacchi** Art Director **Vanessa Todd-Holmes** Director of Print Purchasing **Matt Dryer** Director of Digital Art and Prepress **Michael Gombos** Senior Director of International Publishing and Licensing **Kari Yadro** Director of Custom Programs **Kari Torson** Director of International Licensing **Sean Brice** Director of Trade Sales

DISNEY PUBLISHING WORLDWIDE GLOBAL MAGAZINES, COMICS AND PARTWORKS

PUBLISHER **Lynn Waggoner** • EDITORIAL TEAM **Bianca Coletti** (Director, Magazines), **Guido Frazzini** (Director, Comics), **Carlotta Quattrocolo** (Executive Editor), **Stefano Ambrosio** (Executive Editor, New IP), **Camilla Vedove** (Senior Manager, Editorial Development), **Behnoosh Khalili** (Senior Editor), **Julie Dorris** (Senior Editor), **Mina Riazi** (Assistant Editor), **Gabriela Capasso** (Assistant Editor) • DESIGN **Enrico Soave** (Senior Designer) • ART **Ken Shue** (VP, Global Art), **Manny Mederos** (Senior Illustration Manager, Comics and Magazines), **Roberto Santillo** (Creative Director), **Marco Ghiglione** (Creative Manager), **Stefano Attardi** (Illustration Manager) • PORTFOLIO MANAGEMENT **Olivia Ciancarelli** (Director) • BUSINESS & MARKETING **Mariantonietta Galla** (Senior Manager, Franchise), **Virpi Korhonen** (Editorial Manager)

FROZEN ADVENTURES: SNOWY STORIES

Published by Dark Horse Books
A division of Dark Horse Comics LLC
10956 SE Main Street, Milwaukie, OR 97222

DarkHorse.com

To find a comics shop in your area, visit comicshoplocator.com

First edition: February 2020 | ISBN 978-1-50671-471-4
Digital ISBN 978-1-50671-474-5

10 9 8 7 6 5 4 3 2 1
Printed in China

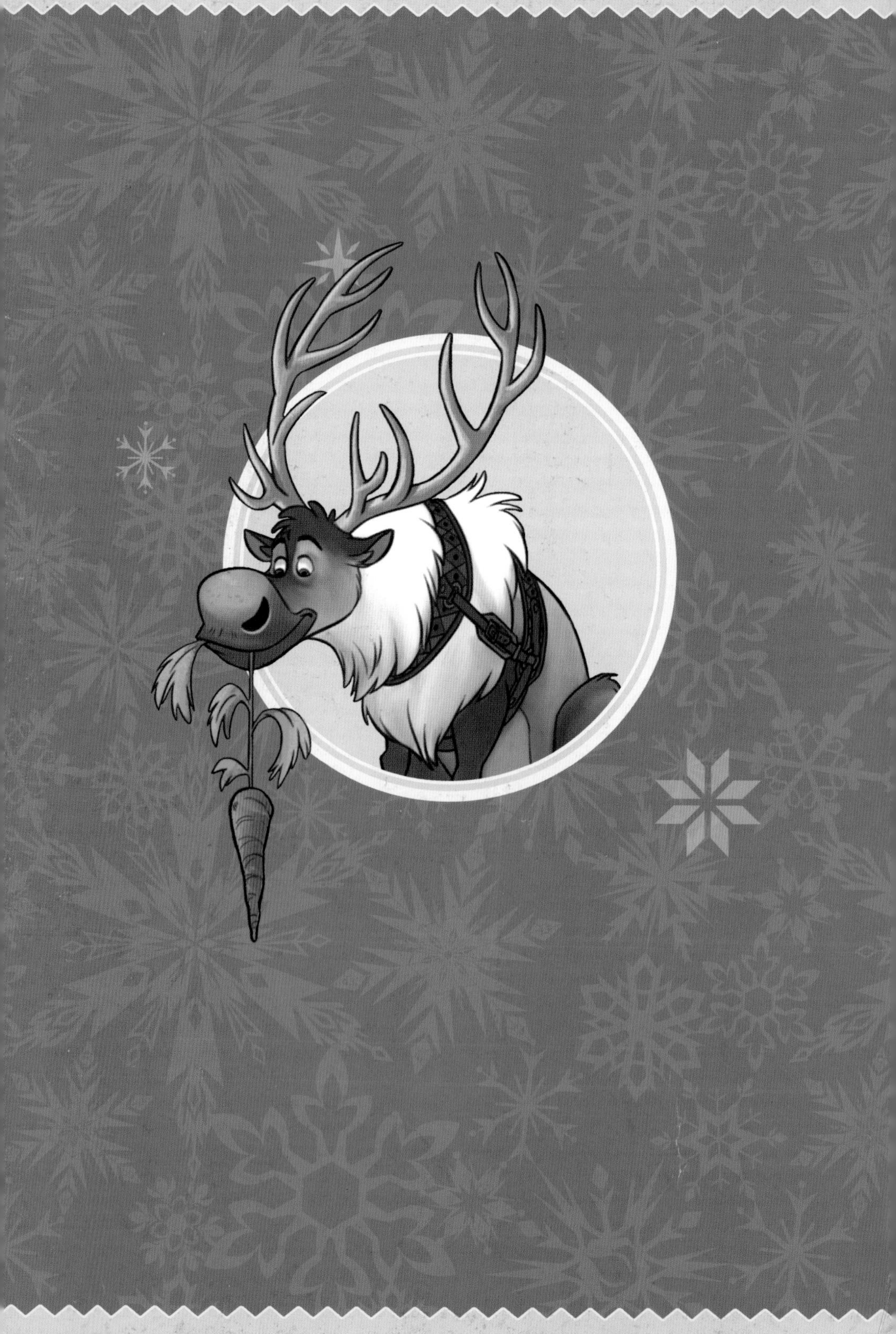

LUR THIEF

HELLO KAI! HOW ARE YOU THIS MORNING?

VERY WELL, THANK YOU OLAF!

HI GERDA, NICE TO SEE YOU!

NICE TO SEE YOU TOO, OLAF.

Script: Georgia Ball; Layouts: Benedetta Barone; Inks: Michela Cacciatore, Elisabetta Melaranci;
Colors: Kat Maximenko, Manuela Nerolini, Cecilia Giumento, Alessandra Bracaglia, Alessandro Russato, Julia Pinchuk; Letters: AndWorld Design

HELLO THERE!

I'VE NEVER SEEN YOU BEFORE. YOU MUST BE NEW!

I'M OLAF! AND YOU ARE...

UM, UH-- THORD!

I WAS ASKED TO CLEAN IN HERE. VERY DUSTY!

OH! THAT SOUNDS LIKE FUN.

UH, WELL... YES! VERY FUN.

CAN I HELP?

OH! UM, FINE...

...WHY DON'T YOU TAKE THIS TO THE LIVING ROOM AND GIVE IT A SHINE? IT WILL BE EASIER TO CLEAN IN THE LIGHT.

OO! THERE'S LIGHT BY THE WINDOW, MAYBE I SHOULD CLEAN THE BEAR OVER THERE--

THERE'S SO MUCH *MORE* LIGHT IN THE LIVING ROOM! I'D GO MYSELF BUT I HAVE TO DUST THE SHELVES YOU CAN'T REACH...

WHERE ARE YOU TAKING THE PEWTER BEAR, OLAF?

WHO?

TO THE LIVING ROOM! I'M HELPING MY NEW FRIEND THORD CLEAN THE ART GALLERY.

I THINK WE MIGHT HAVE AN UNINVITED GUEST...

UH-OH...

I FOUND THIS MAN SNEAKING AROUND THE CASTLE WITHOUT PERMISSION, QUEEN ELSA--

IT'S MY NEW FRIEND, THORD!

--AND HE WAS TRYING TO RUN OFF WITH *THIS*.

THAT'S A VERY SERIOUS CHARGE. WHY IS THIS MAP SO IMPORTANT TO YOU?

I AM THORD FROM THE KASKADER MOUNTAINS--A DISTANT RELATION TO YOUR FAMILY AND THE TRUE HEIR TO THE THRONE OF ARENDELLE!

I'M SORRY, BUT THAT'S IMPOSSIBLE. ELSA IS QUEEN OF ARENDELLE.

THAT'S WHAT *YOU* SAY!

I KNOW BETTER. AND ONCE I FIND OUT WHAT THAT MAP LEADS TO--

--NOTHING WILL STOP ME FROM GETTING WHAT I WANT.

WHAT *DOES* IT LEAD TO?

THE SOURCE OF *OUR* FAMILY'S POWER--*YOUR* POWERS, QUEEN ELSA!

THE MAP'S SECRET WILL GIVE THEM TO ME--AND IF YOU WERE *MEANT* TO BE QUEEN, YOU *SHOULD* ALREADY KNOW.

WHAT SHOULD WE DO WITH HIM, QUEEN ELSA?

I THINK IT WOULD BE BEST TO HOLD HIM FOR NOW...

THORD IS GOING TO STAY WITH US!

DON'T WORRY, I'LL KEEP YOU COMPANY.

"...UNTIL WE CAN LEARN MORE ABOUT THIS MAP."

KRISTOFF'S HOME!!

QUEEN ELSA! PRINCESS ANNA!

IT'S GOOD TO SEE YOU TOO, GRAND PABBIE.

YOU LOOK UPSET, HAS SOMETHING HAPPENED?

WE NEED YOUR HELP DECIPHERING THIS MAP.

SOMEONE TOLD US IT'S *REALLY* IMPORTANT.

AH, YES...

...LONG AGO, YOUR GREAT-GREAT-GREAT GRANDMOTHER WAS GIVEN A BRONZE HORN CALLED THE ELFENBEN LUR AS A GIFT OF FRIENDSHIP FROM A NEIGHBORING KINGDOM.

"IT BELONGED TO YOUR FAMILY FOR MANY YEARS UNTIL THE DAY IT MYSTERIOUSLY DISAPPEARED."

"THIS MAP CLAIMS TO LEAD TO THE PLACE THE LUR IS HIDDEN."

WHY IS THIS HORN SO IMPORTANT?

LEGEND SAYS THAT THE LUR REVEALS THE SOURCE OF THE STRENGTH OF ARENDELLE'S ROYAL FAMILY.

HOW CAN IT DO THAT?

I'M NOT SURE.

DOES IT HAVE SOMETHING TO DO WITH ELSA'S POWERS?

I WISH I KNEW!

THORD SEEMS TO THINK THE HORN WILL GIVE HIM POWERS LIKE MINE.

PERHAPS HE CAME TO *THAT* CONCLUSION ON HIS OWN.

BUT EITHER WAY, THE ELFENBEN LUR IS A SIGNIFICANT PIECE OF YOUR FAMILY'S ANCIENT HISTORY--

--AND IT HAS GREAT VALUE.

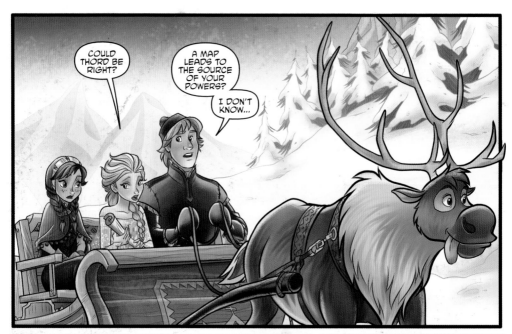

COULD THORD BE RIGHT?

A MAP LEADS TO THE SOURCE OF YOUR POWERS?

I DON'T KNOW...

I'D LIKE TO TALK TO HIM AGAIN...

WHAT'S GOING ON?

QUEEN ELSA--

--THORD ESCAPED!

I'M SO SORRY, QUEEN ELSA...

...HE'S JUST SO WILY.

IT'S ALL RIGHT. HE DOES SEEM RATHER SLIPPERY.

HE LEFT WITHOUT SAYING GOOD-BYE!

HE RAN OFF YELLING HE WOULD "FIND THE LUR ON HIS OWN..."

DO YOU KNOW WHAT HE MEANT?

I HAVE AN IDEA.

HE'LL HAVE A TOUGH TIME DOING IT WITHOUT THE MAP.

I GUESS HE'S TRYING TO DO IT FROM MEMORY.

GRAND PABBIE SAID THE LUR IS AN IMPORTANT PART OF OUR FAMILY HISTORY.

WHAT IF IT *COULD* TELL US MORE ABOUT OUR ANCESTORS OR WHERE MY POWERS CAME FROM?

YOU'RE RIGHT ELSA...

...WE NEED TO FIND THE LUR BEFORE THORD DOES.

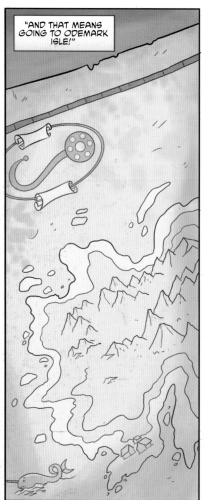

"AND THAT MEANS GOING TO ODEMARK ISLE!"

After two days traveling by sea...

LOOK!

THE NARWHAL PODS ARE MIGRATING NORTH!

On the third day they reach the largest settlement on Odemärk Isle...

WELCOME TO KJEDELIG, QUEEN ELSA! THE LAST TIME I SAW YOU AND PRINCESS ANNA, YOU WERE BARELY KNEE-HIGH.

YOU WERE A GOOD FRIEND TO OUR FATHER, REID. I HOPE YOU CAN HELP US NOW.

THESE LOOK LIKE THE ROCKS OFF THE BAY WHERE THE NARWHALS MIGRATE. THEY SAY THERE ARE UNDERGROUND CAVERNS THERE.

THIS IS A VERY OLD MAP, BUT I THINK I RECOGNIZE THE AREA.

YOU'LL HAVE TO TRAVEL A LONG STRETCH OF ICY GROUND TO GET THERE.

YOU'LL NEED SUPPLIES.

I'LL HELP YOU LOAD THEM ON SVEN.

I'LL LEND YOU A SLED.

"YOU'D BEST LEAVE EARLY, QUEEN ELSA.

"YOU HAVE A LONG, COLD JOURNEY AHEAD OF YOU."

I THINK THOSE CLIFFS SHOULD BE ON OUR LEFT. BETTER FIND MY COMPASS...

WE SHOULD CHECK THE MAP AGAIN.

OLAF, CAN YOU HOLD THE MAP OPEN WHILE I HELP ANNA FIND THE COMPASS?

WHY DON'T YOU JUST GIVE *US* THE MAP?

WE'D BE HAPPY TO TAKE IT FROM YOU, IF YOU INSIST ON MAKING THINGS DIFFICULT.

NO ONE HAS TO GET HURT.

WE AGREE! ALL WE WANT IS THE MAP.

MY BROTHERS WILL MAKE SURE YOU STAY HERE LONG ENOUGH FOR THORD TO FIND THE LUR FIRST.

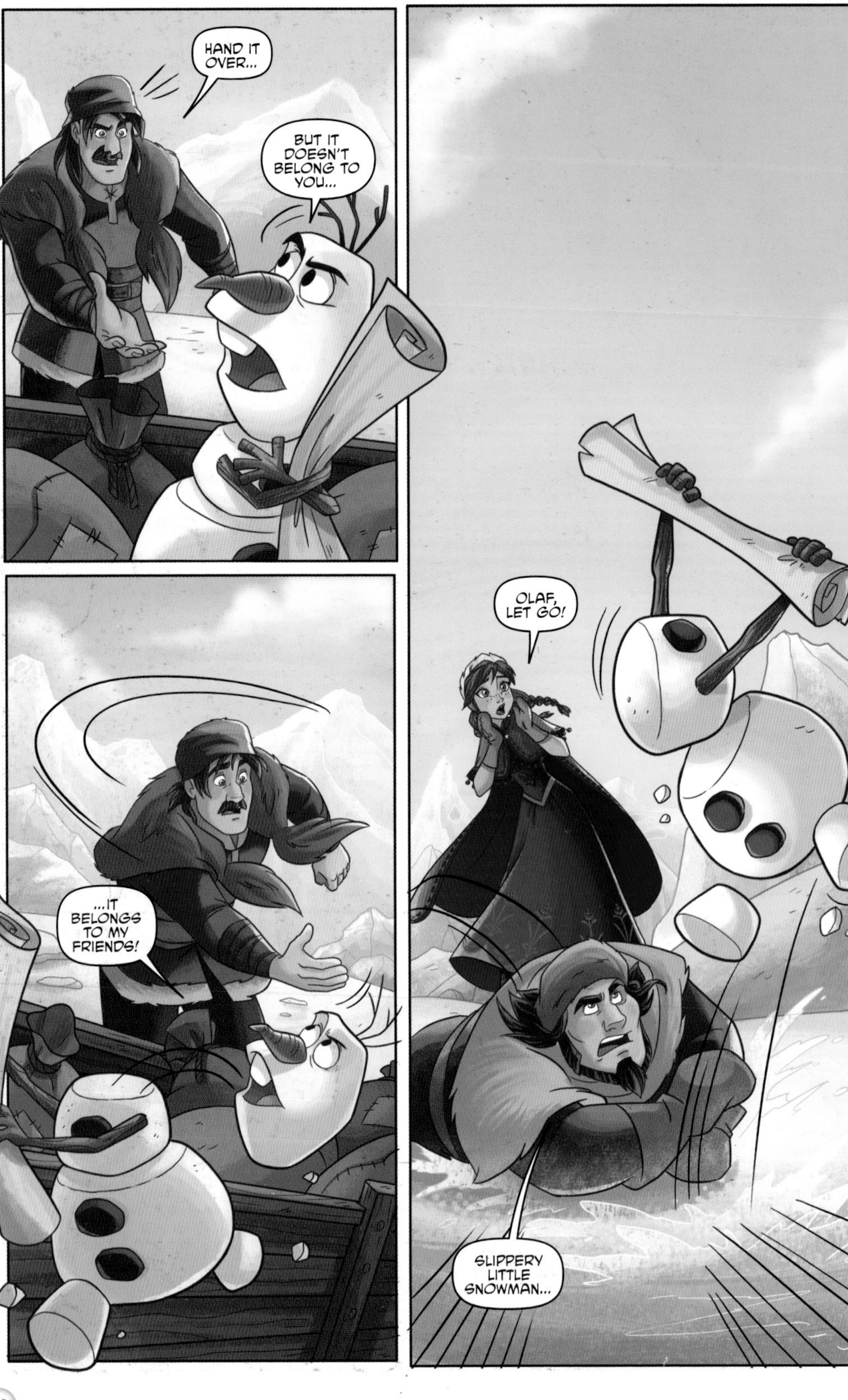
HAND IT OVER...
BUT IT DOESN'T BELONG TO YOU...
...IT BELONGS TO MY FRIENDS!
OLAF, LET GO!
SLIPPERY LITTLE SNOWMAN...

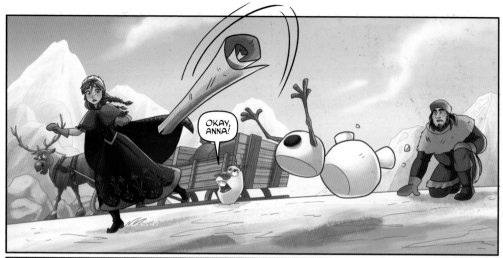

OKAY, ANNA!

SMART DECISION. THANKS FOR SEEING THINGS OUR WAY.

GRRRR

GRRRR

GRRRR

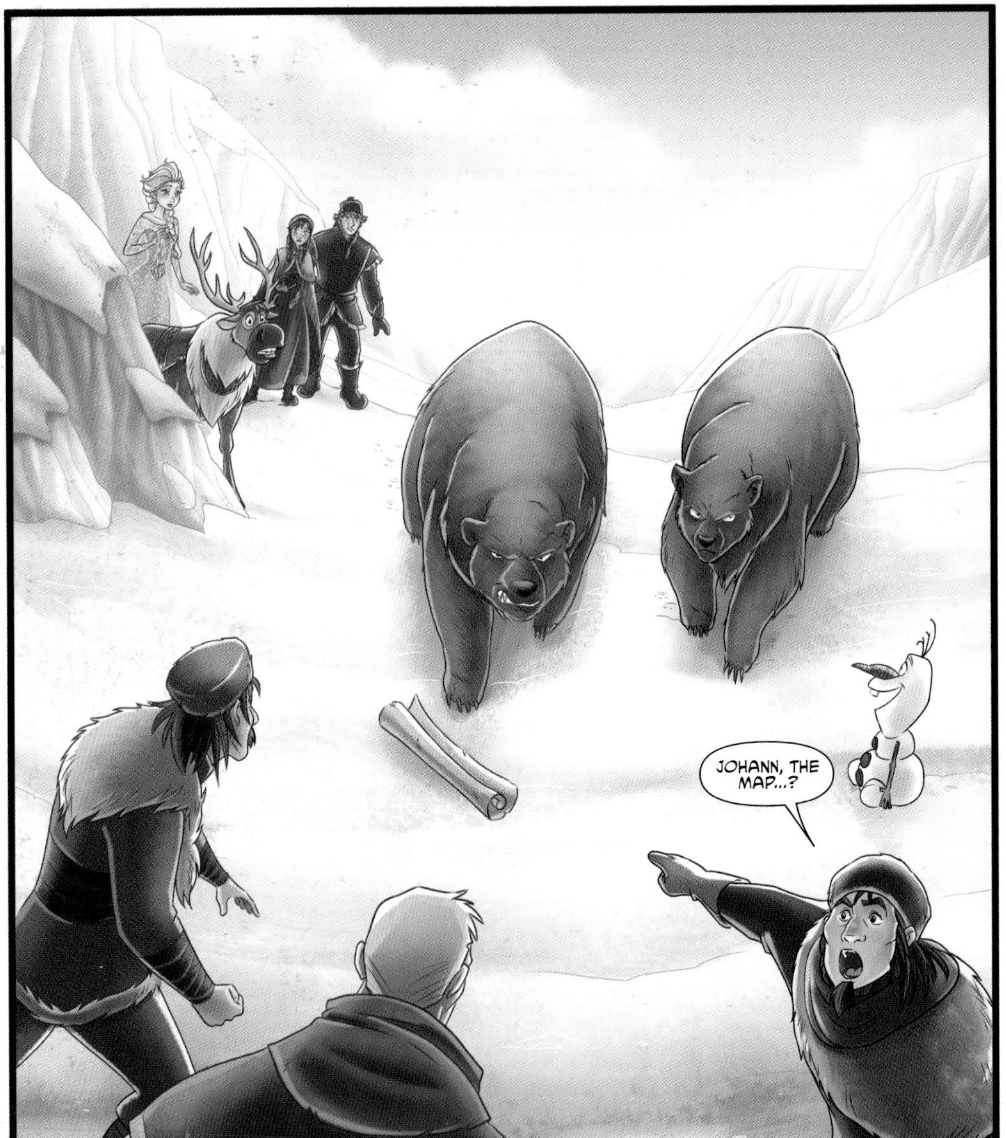
JOHANN, THE MAP...?

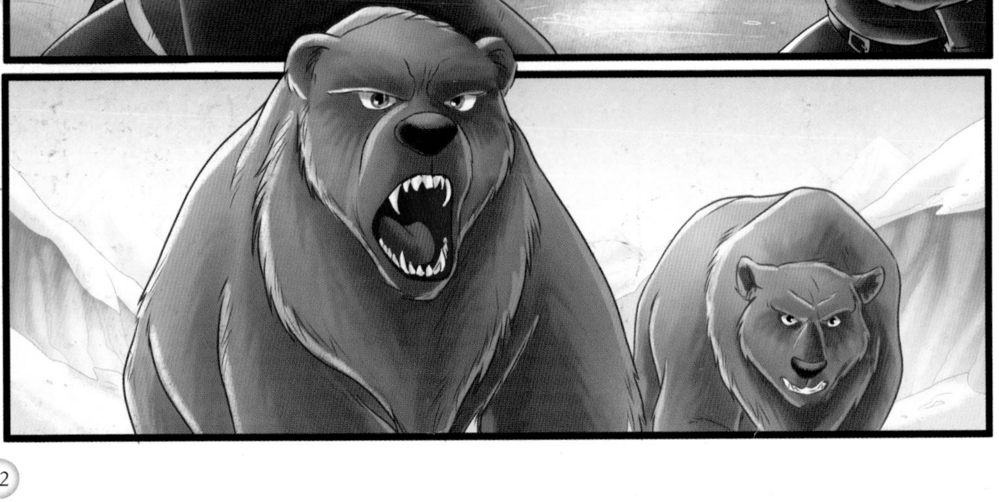

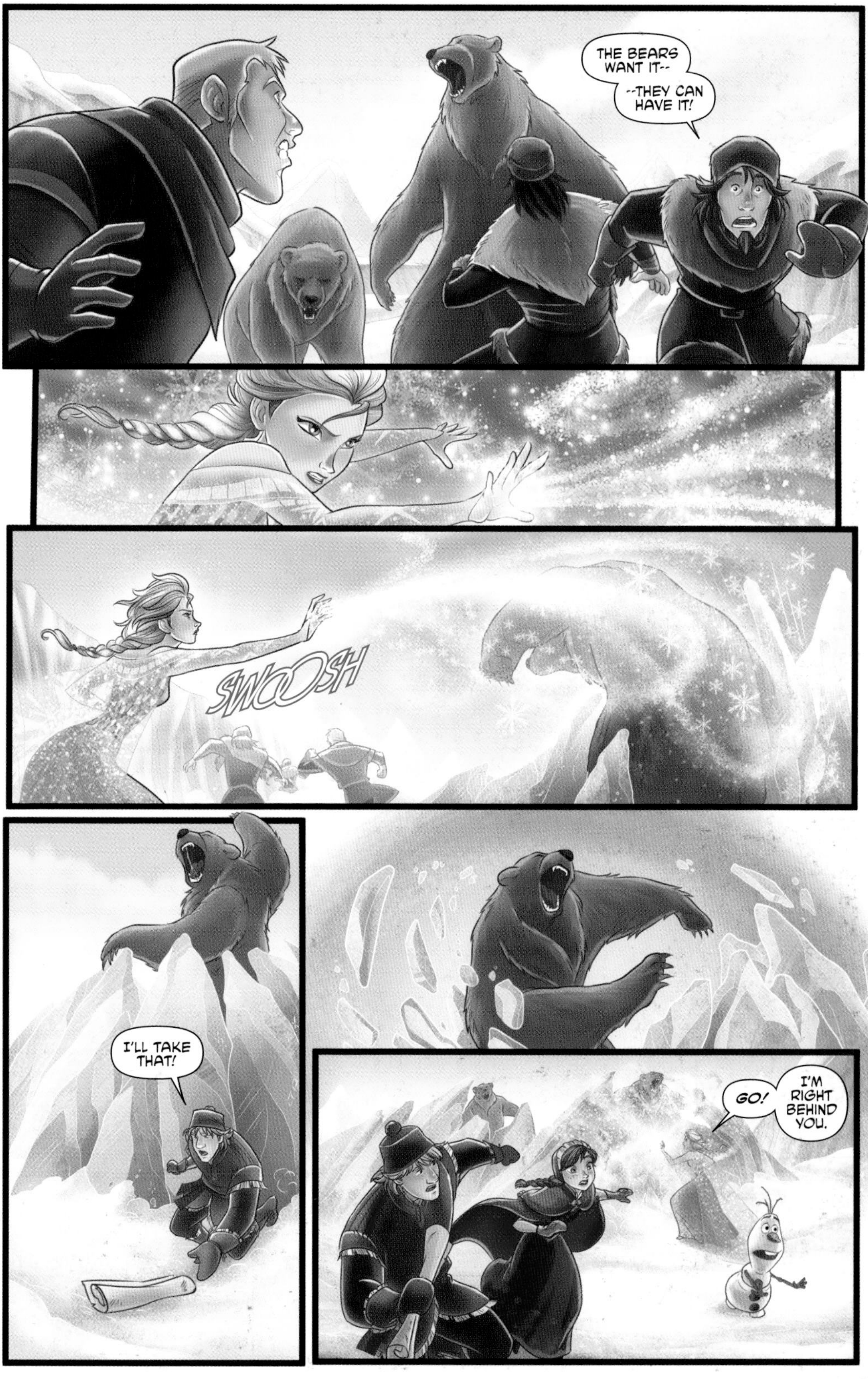
THE BEARS WANT IT--
--THEY CAN HAVE IT!
SWOOSH
I'LL TAKE THAT!
GO!
I'M RIGHT BEHIND YOU.

A few minutes later...

ANY SIGN OF THOSE MEN, KRISTOFF?

NO... I THINK THEY KNEW I WAS ABOUT TO TAKE ON ALL THREE OF THEM AT ONCE--

--BUT MOSTLY THEY WERE AFRAID OF THE BEARS.

WITH GOOD REASON!

WELL, THORD MAY NOT BE ABLE TO GET THERE FIRST WITHOUT THE MAP--

...BUT HE COULD STILL BE FOLLOWING US!

WHERE? I DON'T SEE HIM!

MAYBE HE'S NOT FOLLOWING US *THAT* CLOSE, OLAF.

I DON'T KNOW WHY THORD IS TRYING SO HARD, THE LUR IS JUST AN ORDINARY HORN!

HOW DO YOU KNOW, ANNA?

YOUR POWERS ARE PART OF *YOU*--NOT SOMETHING YOU CAN LEARN FROM A HORN.

STILL... I'M CURIOUS WHAT WE *CAN* LEARN FROM IT.

LOOK AT THOSE ROCKS UP AHEAD!

THE MAP SAYS THERE'S AN ENTRANCE AROUND HERE SOMEWHERE...

REALLY? BECAUSE ALL I SEE IS THIS BIG HOLE.

THAT MUST BE IT!

IT'S A BIT OF A TIGHT FIT...

...WHAT IS THAT???

IT'S CARVED WITH ANCIENT SYMBOLS OF PROTECTION.

THERE IS A WAY IN. BUT IT'S SHUT UP TIGHT!

THE WAY THE POLE FITS IN THE GROUND MAKES ME THINK IT CAN BE LOWERED SOMEHOW, IF IT JUST HAD A LITTLE MORE WEIGHT...

WAIT A MINUTE...

...ISN'T THIS OUR FAMILY CREST?

MAYBE THESE ARE INSTRUCTIONS FOR US--THAT IS, SPECIFICALLY FOR SOMEONE IN OUR FAMILY?

IT DOESN'T MAKE ANY SENSE TO ME.

PROTECTION SYMBOL, WAVY LINES, DOORWAY, CREST AND TIPPING JAR...

IT LOOKS LIKE A PUZZLE!

MAYBE IF WE REARRANGE THE TILES...

...LET'S START WITH THE CREST!

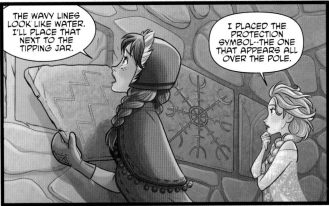

THE WAVY LINES LOOK LIKE WATER. I'LL PLACE THAT NEXT TO THE TIPPING JAR.

I PLACED THE PROTECTION SYMBOL--THE ONE THAT APPEARS ALL OVER THE POLE.

I DON'T THINK IT MEANS "PROTECTION" THIS TIME--I THINK IT REFERS TO THE CARVINGS ON THE POLE.

WE SHOULD POUR WATER INTO THE CARVINGS... TO OPEN THE DOOR!

BUT THE POLE IS UPRIGHT. HOW ARE WE GOING TO GET WATER INTO VERTICAL CARVINGS?

I THINK I KNOW!

RAINBOWS!

WHIIRRRRRRRR

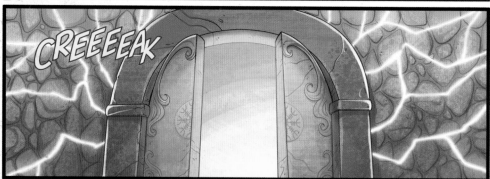

CREEEEAK

IT WORKED!

THAT WAS AMAZING! I WISH WE COULD DO IT ALL OVER AGAIN...

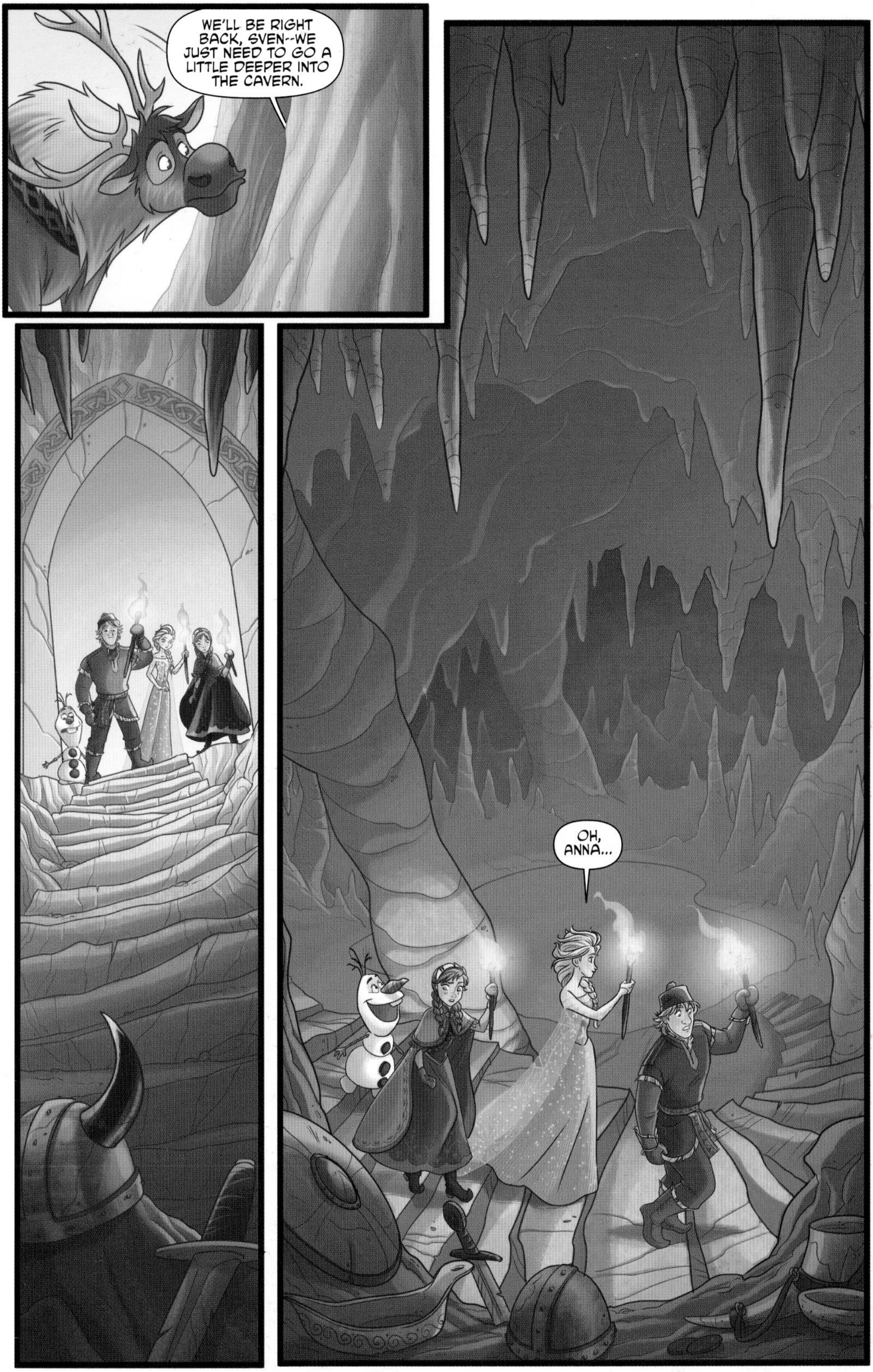
WE'LL BE RIGHT BACK, SVEN--WE JUST NEED TO GO A LITTLE DEEPER INTO THE CAVERN.
OH, ANNA...

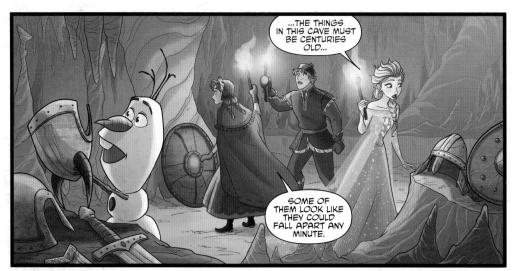

...THE THINGS IN THIS CAVE MUST BE CENTURIES OLD...

SOME OF THEM LOOK LIKE THEY COULD FALL APART ANY MINUTE.

CHINK

IT'S *THE LUR*--WE FOUND IT!

ELSA, OVER HERE!

IT'S LOVELY...

AND NOW IT'S MINE!

⸬GASP⸬

FWEEP

I USED THE HORN, IT SHOULD HAVE GIVEN ME ICE POWERS BY NOW!

WHAT'S THE MATTER WITH THIS THING...

DOES THORD KNOW HOW A HORN WORKS?

BECAUSE I HAVE NO IDEA.

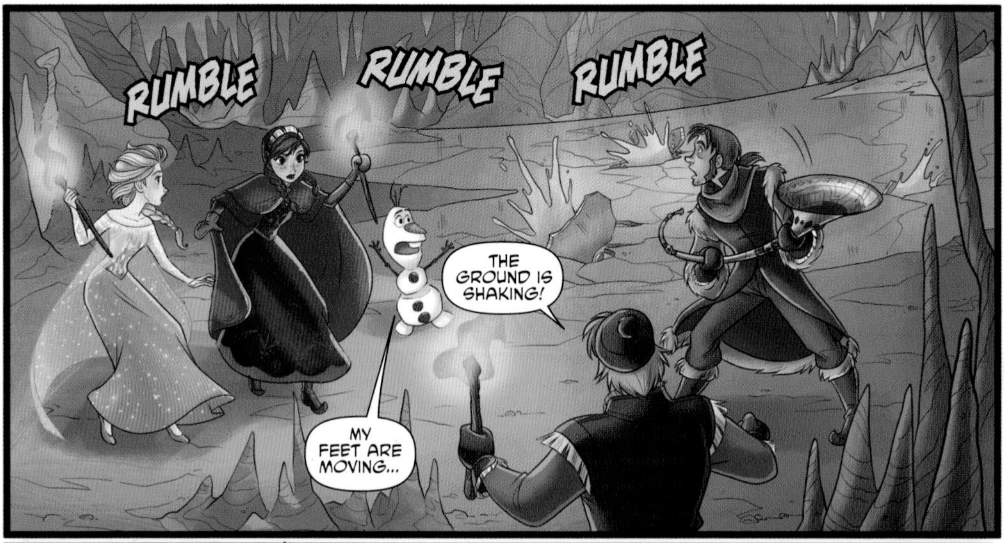
RUMBLE
RUMBLE
RUMBLE
THE GROUND IS SHAKING!
MY FEET ARE MOVING...

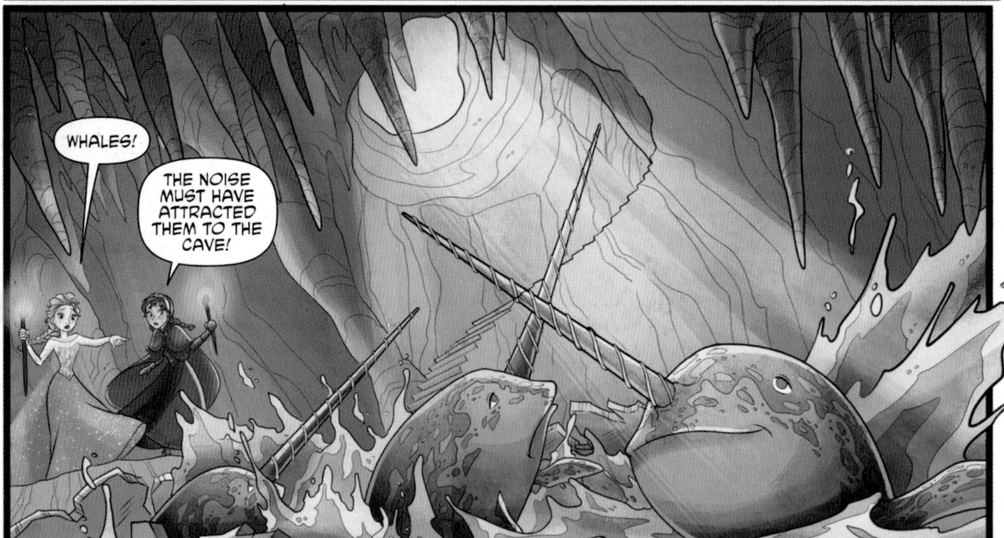
WHALES!
THE NOISE MUST HAVE ATTRACTED THEM TO THE CAVE!

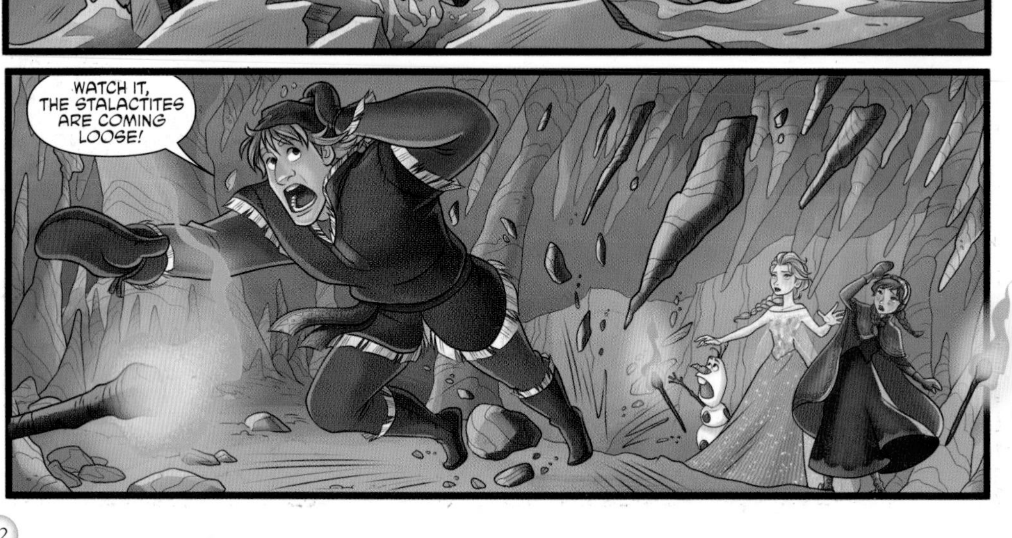
WATCH IT, THE STALACTITES ARE COMING LOOSE!

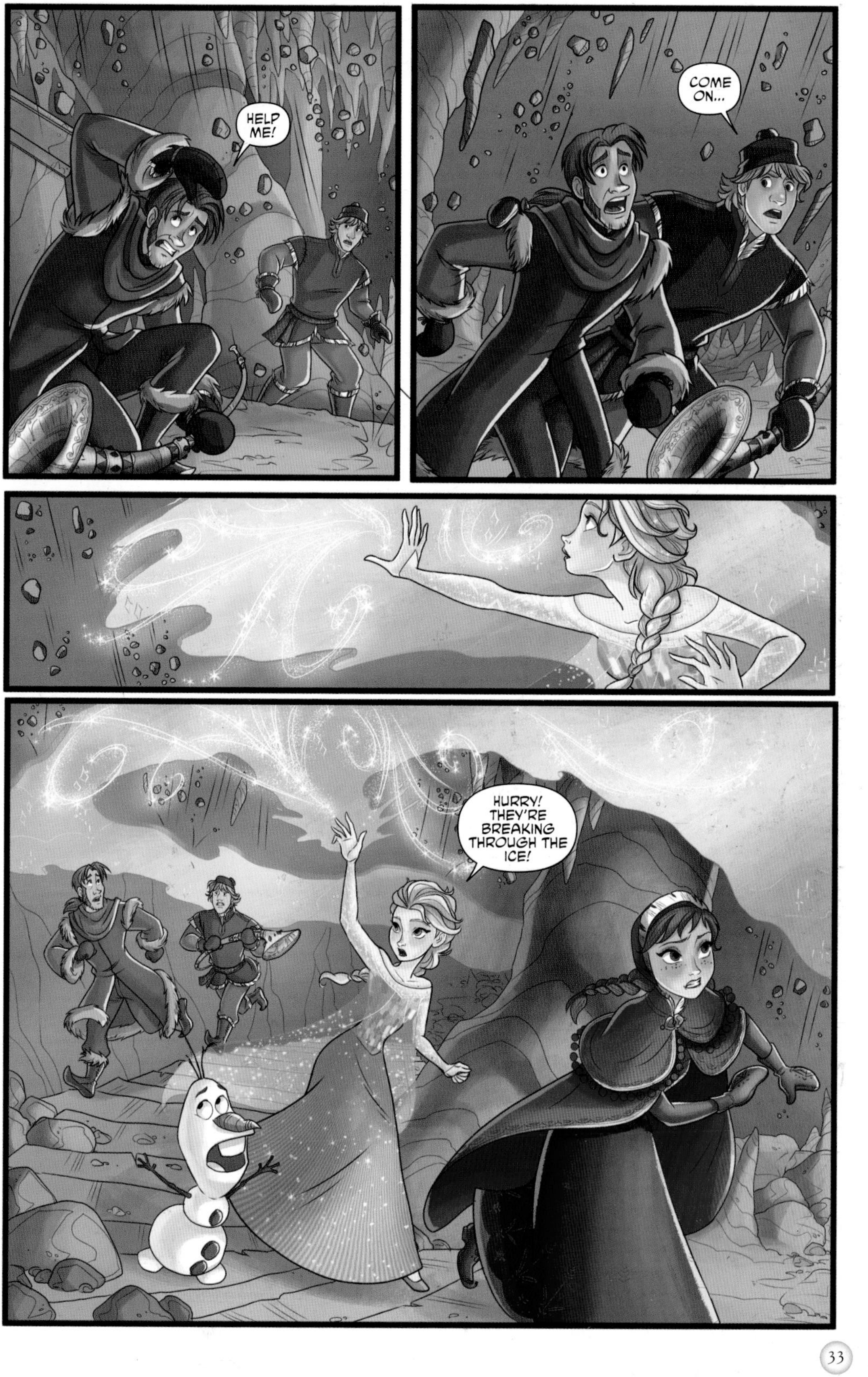
HELP ME!
COME ON...
HURRY! THEY'RE BREAKING THROUGH THE ICE!

WE'RE ALL OUT SAFE, AND SO IS THE LUR!

LOOK AT THE CARVINGS ON IT, ANNA...

...GRAND PABBIE SAID THIS HORN WAS GIVEN TO OUR GREAT-GREAT-GREAT GRANDMOTHER...

...DO YOU THINK THAT'S HER SISTER?

THEY LOOK SO MUCH ALIKE!

NOW I KNOW WHAT HE MEANT-- THE STRENGTH OF OUR FAMILY DOESN'T COME FROM A HORN...

...IT'S ALWAYS COME FROM OUR LOVE FOR EACH OTHER!

And so the Elfenben Lur is returned safely to Arendelle...

Where Anna makes a discovery in the library...

I SEARCHED THE RECORD BOOKS UNTIL I FOUND A MATCH.

SEE? IT'S THE SAME DRAWING THAT'S ON THE LUR.

THERE REALLY *WAS* A LOT WE COULD LEARN FROM A HORN!

SPEAKING OF THE LUR, WHAT HAPPENED TO THORD?

HE'S FINALLY IN HIS RIGHTFUL PLACE--

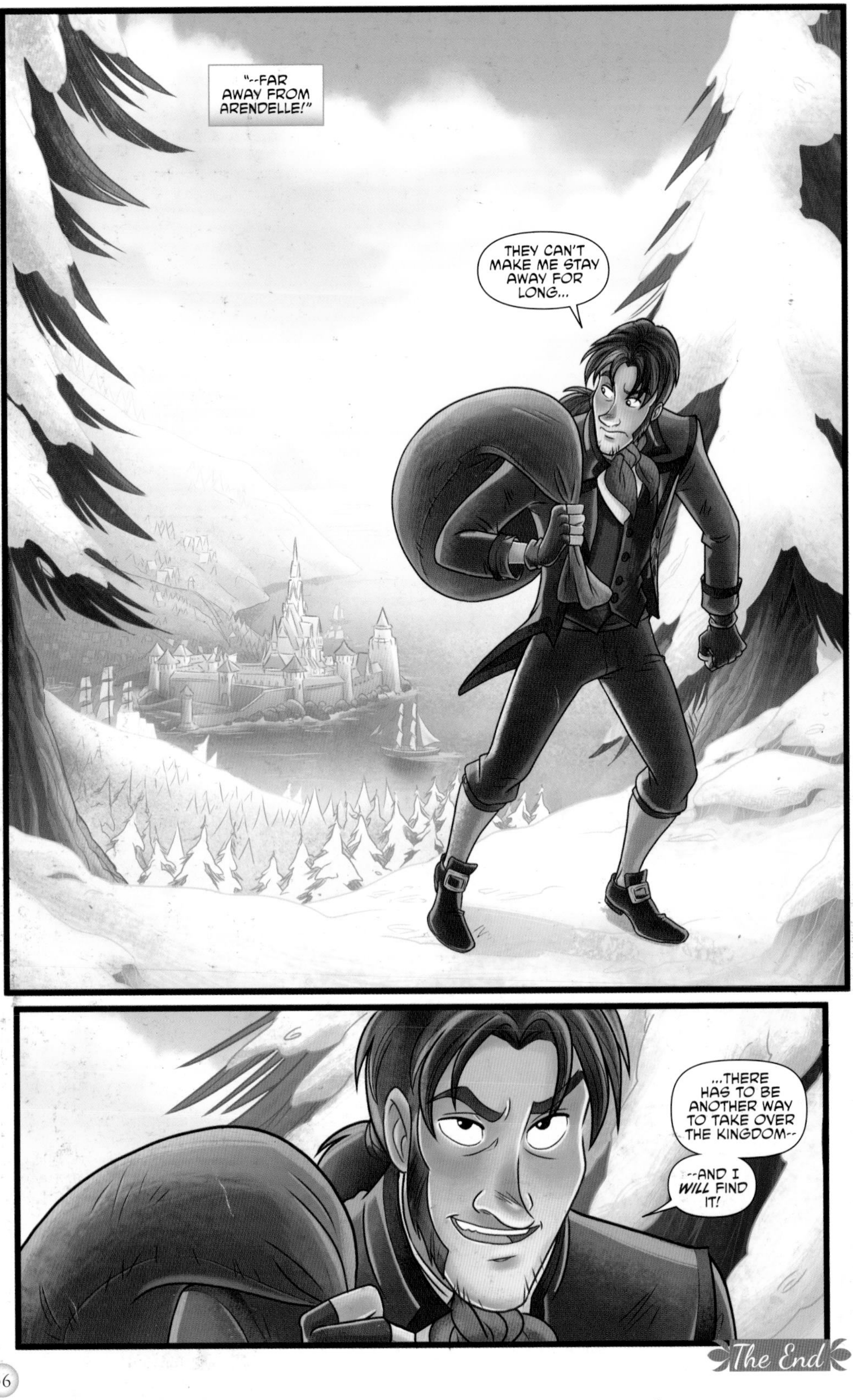
"--FAR AWAY FROM ARENDELLE!"
THEY CAN'T MAKE ME STAY AWAY FOR LONG...
...THERE HAS TO BE ANOTHER WAY TO TAKE OVER THE KINGDOM--
--AND I WILL FIND IT!
The End

The Warmest Scarf Ever

Manuscript: Tea Orsi; Layout and cleanup: Nicoletta Baldari; Color: Dario Calabria

WINTER SURPRISE

KRISTOFF AND HIS REINDEER SVEN JUST SOLD THEIR ICE FOR QUEEN ELSA'S CORONATION AND ARE NOW GOING BACK TO THE NORTH MOUNTAIN...

I'VE GOT TO TELL YOU, BUDDY...I LOVE SUMMER!

THE TEMPERATURE IS HIGH, THE SUN BURNS, PEOPLE GET HOT...AND THEY NEED A LOT OF ICE!

THE ICE *WE* SELL!

SOMETIMES I THINK WE'RE WAY TOO LUCKY, YOU KNOW, SVEN?

THAT VERY MOMENT, ELSA RUNS UP THE NORTH MOUNTAIN...

...WITH HER MAGIC AT MAXIMUM POWER!

FSSSSSSSH

WAIT A SECOND... WHAT...

FWUMP

REMIND ME TO KEEP MY MOUTH SHUT, SVEN... ≈SIGH≈

Writer: Alessandro Ferrari Artist: Iboix Estudi
Colorist: Charles Pickens Letterer: Patrick Brosseau

The End

WHERE'S MY HEAD?

Writer: Alessandro Ferrari Artist: Iboix Estudi
Colorist: Charles Pickens Letterer: Patrick Brosseau

THE NORTH MOUNTAIN. ANNA AND HER NEW FRIENDS ARE WALKING TO ELSA'S ICE PALACE...

ARE YOU SURE IT'S THIS WAY, OLAF?

SURE! STRAIGHT AHEAD!

PLEASE, DON'T GET LEFT BEHIND!

DON'T WORRY, ANNA!

THUNK!

HEY! WAIT!

A DARK AND MYSTERIOUS HOLE! I WANNA SEE WHAT'S INSIDE!

I LOVE FLYING!

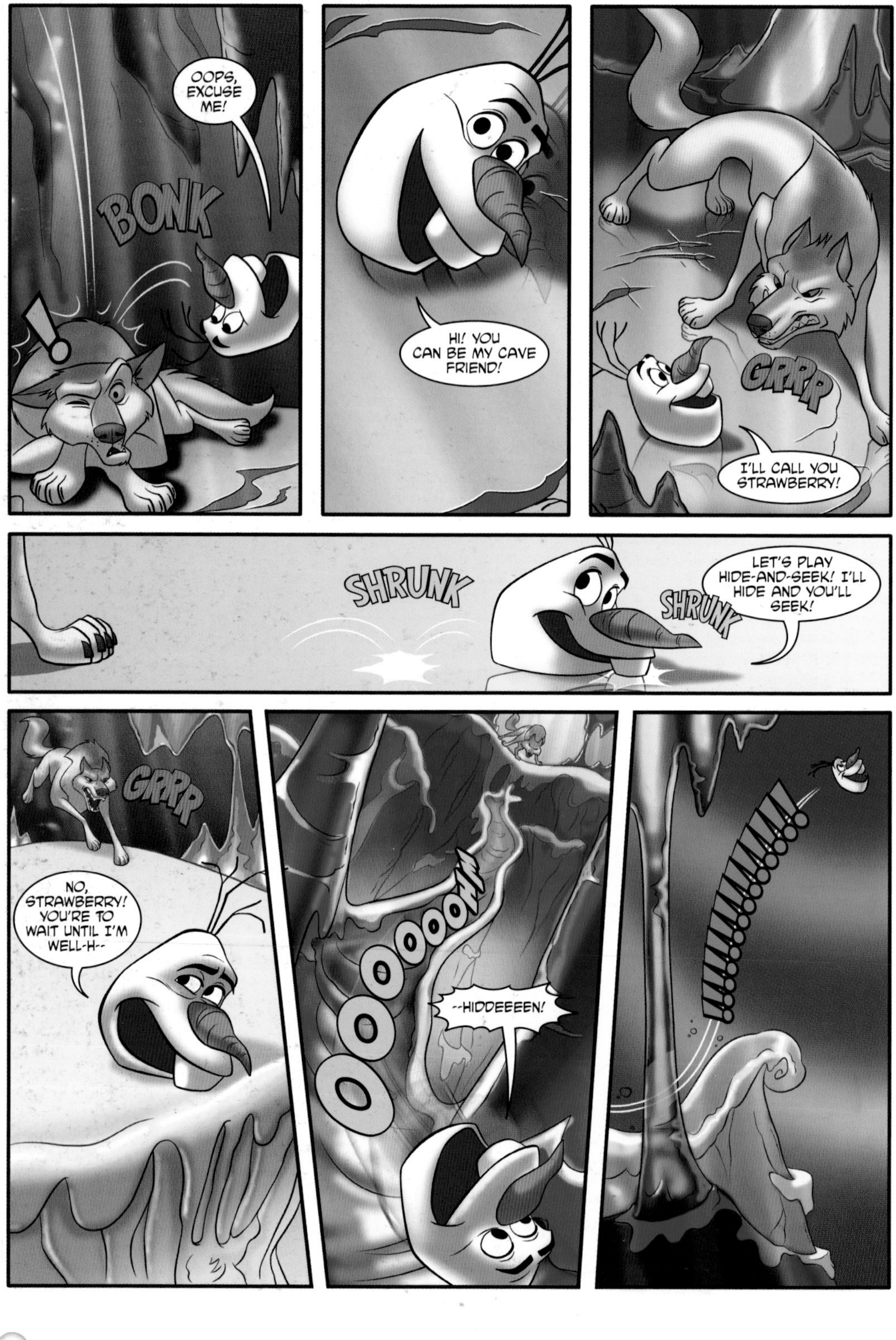
OOPS, EXCUSE ME!
BONK
!
HI! YOU CAN BE MY CAVE FRIEND!
GRRR
I'LL CALL YOU STRAWBERRY!
SHRUNK
SHRUNK
LET'S PLAY HIDE-AND-SEEK! I'LL HIDE AND YOU'LL SEEK!
GRRR
NO, STRAWBERRY! YOU'RE TO WAIT UNTIL I'M WELL-H--
OOOOOOOOHH
--HIDDEEEEN!
!!!!!!!!!!!!!!!

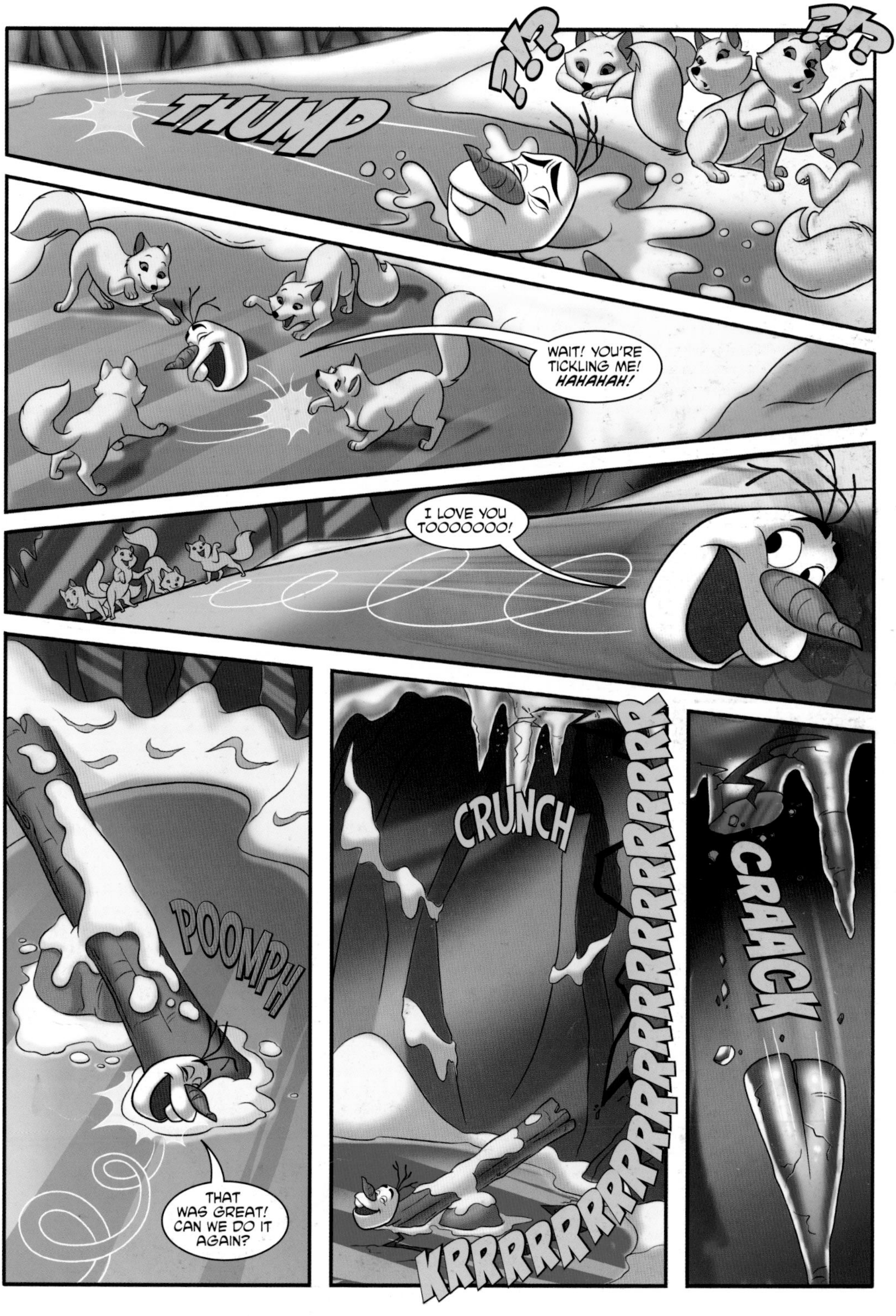
?!?
?!?
THUMP
WAIT! YOU'RE TICKLING ME! HAHAHAH!
I LOVE YOU TOOOOOOO!
POOMPH
THAT WAS GREAT! CAN WE DO IT AGAIN?
CRUNCH
KRRRRRRRRRRRRRRRRRRRRRRRR
CRAACK

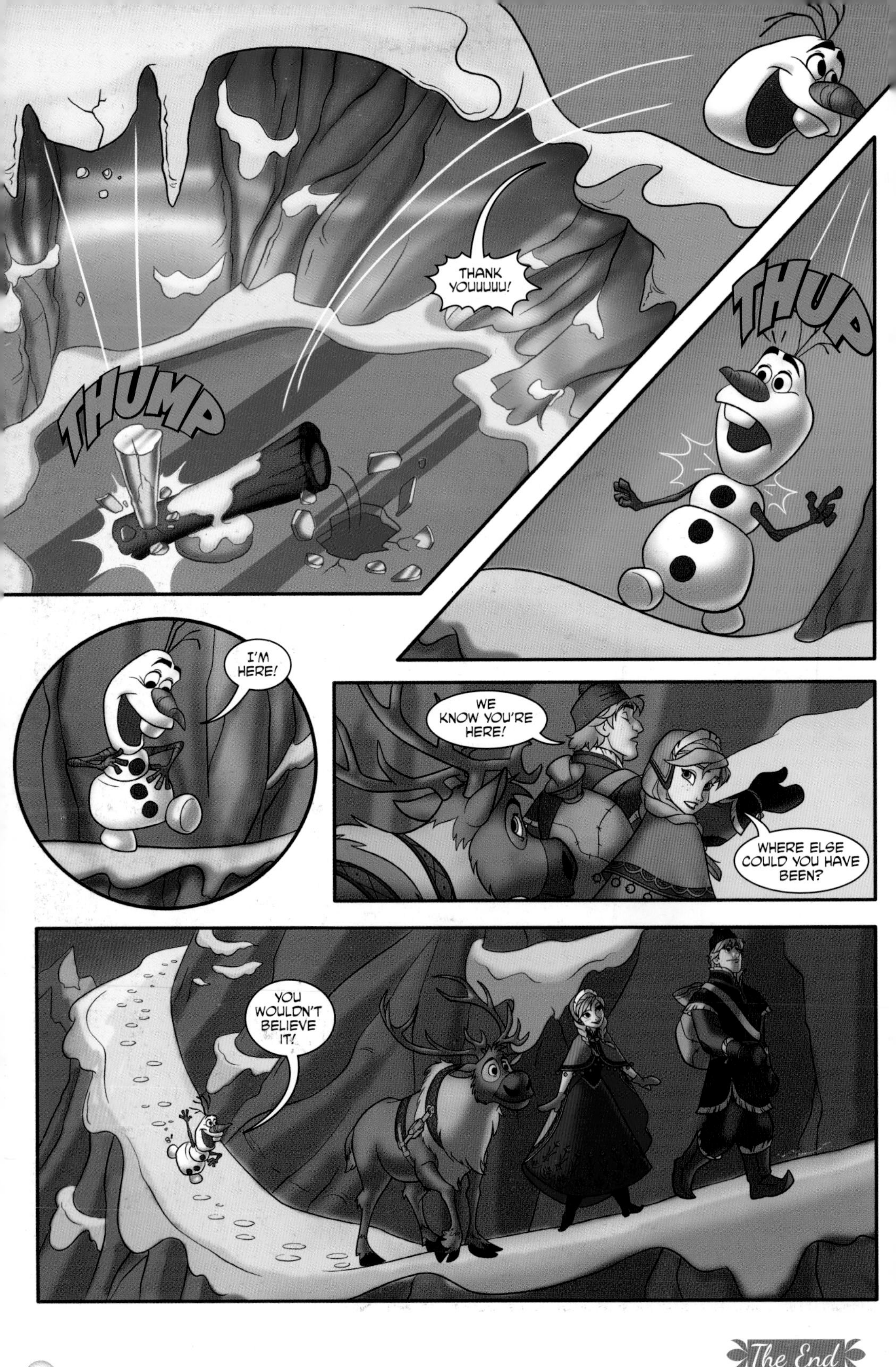
THANK YOUUUUU!
THUMP
THUP
I'M HERE!
WE KNOW YOU'RE HERE!
WHERE ELSE COULD YOU HAVE BEEN?
YOU WOULDN'T BELIEVE IT!

The End

THE BIGGEST TREASURE

ANNA AND ELSA HAVE PLANNED A SPECIAL DAY FOR THE VILLAGE KIDS!

I CAN'T WAIT TO BE AT THE SCHOOL!

I LOVE SCHOOL!

I'M SURE OUR LITTLE FRIENDS WILL LOVE OUR SPECIAL TREASURE HUNT!

IT'S GONNA BE FUN! WE HID THE CLUES THROUGHOUT THE VILLAGE!

BUT...

YIKES! WHERE DID ALL THIS SNOW COME FROM?

IT HAS BEEN SNOWING ALL NIGHT!

ERM... I WAS SO EXCITED THAT I FORGOT TO LOOK OUT THE WINDOW!

ME TOO!

LOOKS LIKE WE'LL HAVE TO RETHINK OUR PLAN!

AND POSTPONE THE TREASURE HUNT TO ANOTHER DAY!

Manuscript: Tea Orsi; Layout: Alberto Zanon; Cleanup: Letizia Algeri, MichelAngela World; Color: MichelAngela World

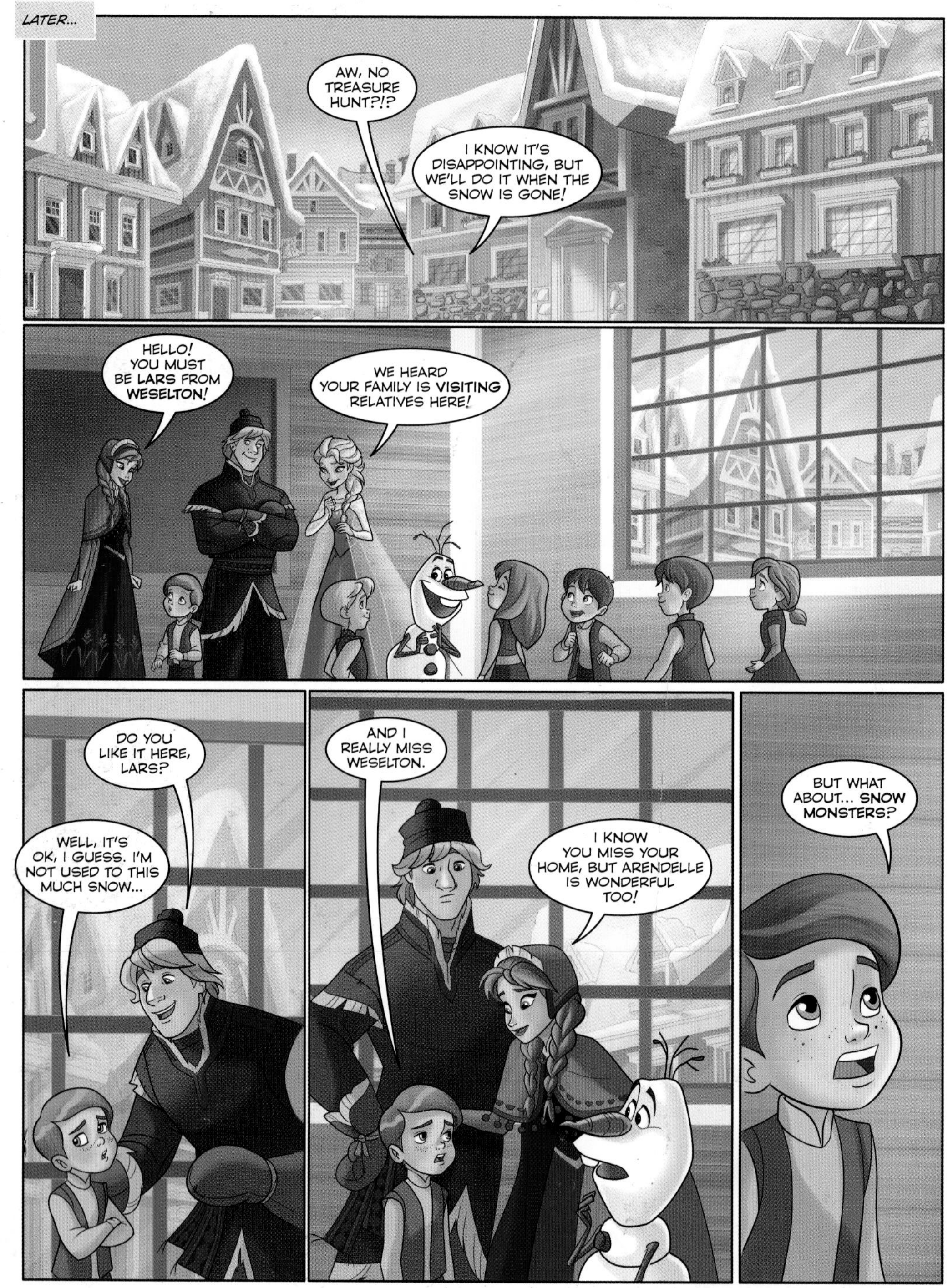
LATER...
AW, NO TREASURE HUNT?!?
I KNOW IT'S DISAPPOINTING, BUT WE'LL DO IT WHEN THE SNOW IS GONE!
HELLO! YOU MUST BE LARS FROM WESELTON!
WE HEARD YOUR FAMILY IS VISITING RELATIVES HERE!
DO YOU LIKE IT HERE, LARS?
WELL, IT'S OK, I GUESS. I'M NOT USED TO THIS MUCH SNOW...
AND I REALLY MISS WESELTON.
I KNOW YOU MISS YOUR HOME, BUT ARENDELLE IS WONDERFUL TOO!
BUT WHAT ABOUT... SNOW MONSTERS?

THE DUKE TOLD US ABOUT THE TERRIBLE SNOW GIANT!

THE DUKE OF WESELTON?!

GASP!

HE SAID THAT HE CAN CATCH YOU WITH HIS HUGE SNOWY CLAWS!

THE DUKE WAS EXAGGERATING, LARS!

HIS NAME IS MARSHMALLOW AND HE'S A FRIEND OF OURS!

BUT THE DUKE SAID THAT HE'S SCARY AND MEAN!

MARSHMALLOW IS NICE!

I DON'T BELIEVE YOU! ANY MONSTER IS SCARY!

IS THAT TRUE, QUEEN ELSA?

IT'S CERTAINLY NOT TRUE ABOUT MARSHMALLOW!

IF ONLY LARS COULD MEET THE **REAL** MARSHMALLOW...

YEAH, THEN HE WOULD CHANGE HIS MIND.

HMM...

MAYBE WE CAN VISIT HIM... BUT FIRST I WANT TO SHOW YOU THE STORY OF MARSHMALLOW. FOLLOW ME!

AND...

ARE YOU GOING TO TELL THE STORY?

YES, YOU'LL SEE.

WATCH CLOSELY!

I'M GOING TO MAKE SOMETHING, AND YOU TELL ME WHAT IT IS!

GASP!

THAT'S MARSHMALLOW!

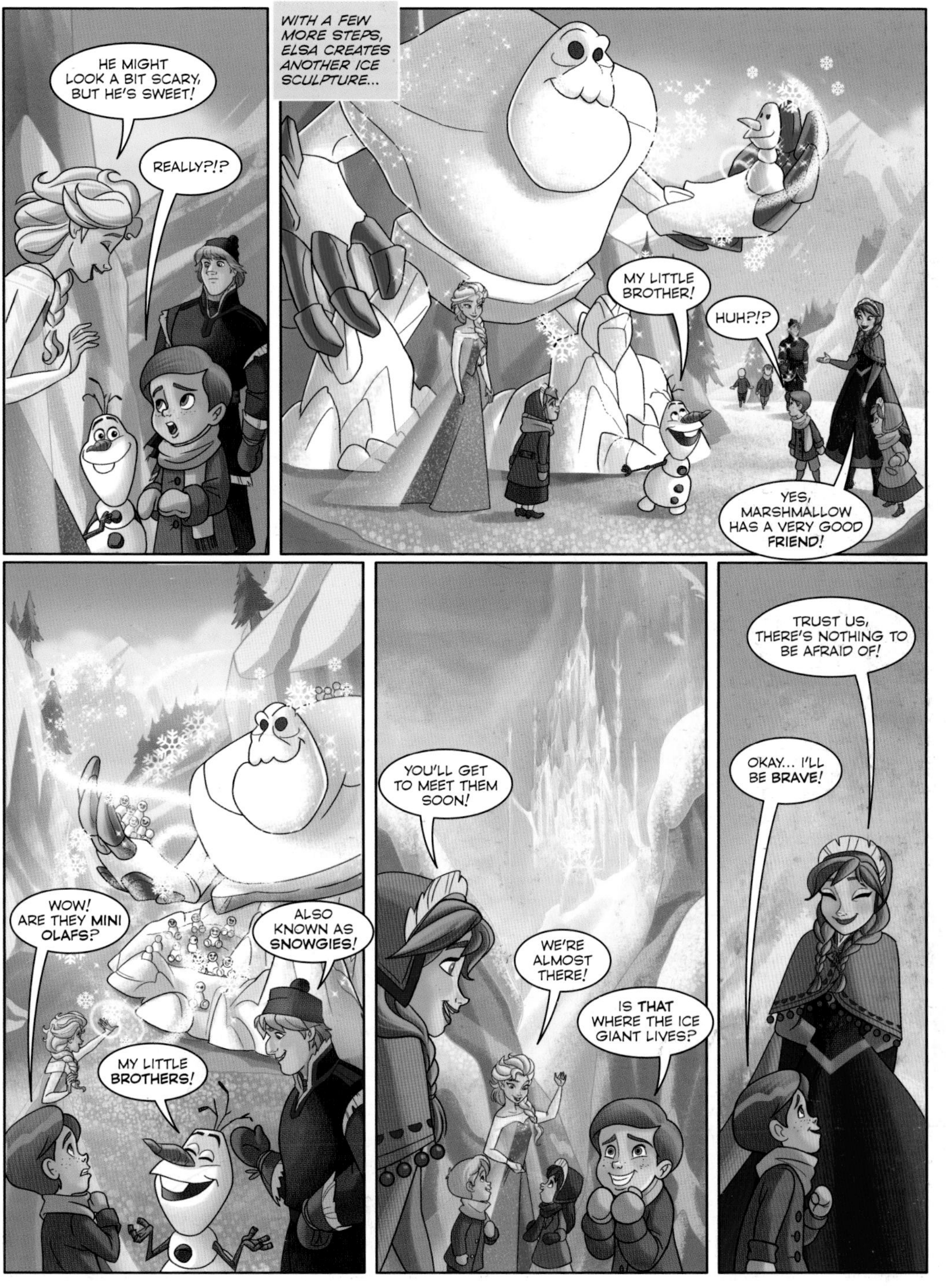
HE MIGHT LOOK A BIT SCARY, BUT HE'S SWEET!
REALLY?!?
WITH A FEW MORE STEPS, ELSA CREATES ANOTHER ICE SCULPTURE...
MY LITTLE BROTHER!
HUH?!?
YES, MARSHMALLOW HAS A VERY GOOD FRIEND!
WOW! ARE THEY MINI OLAFS?
ALSO KNOWN AS SNOWGIES!
MY LITTLE BROTHERS!
YOU'LL GET TO MEET THEM SOON!
WE'RE ALMOST THERE!
IS THAT WHERE THE ICE GIANT LIVES?
TRUST US, THERE'S NOTHING TO BE AFRAID OF!
OKAY... I'LL BE BRAVE!

BUT...

WHERE'S EVERYONE GONE?

YES, WHERE'S MARSHMALLOW? NOW THAT I **WANT** TO MEET HIM?

MAYBE THEY ARE...

SUDDENLY...

GASP!

HEY! I GUESS IT'S HIM!

OH! HELLO MARSHMELLOW

LET'S RIDE HIM TOO!

ARE YOU COMING, LARS?

WHY NOT? IT SOUNDS LIKE **FUN!**

YAY!

LET'S PLAY!

LUCKILY LARS DIDN'T NOTICE, BUT MARSHMALLOW NEARLY SCARED ME THIS TIME...

DON'T WORRY, THIS WILL BE OUR NOT-SO-LITTLE SECRET!

The End

WINTER PICNIC

IT'S A QUIET WINTER DAY IN ARENDELLE...

AND FINALLY ALL THE KIDS HAD A LOVELY PICNIC TOGETHER!

PICNIC? I LOVE PICNICS!

I WISH WE COULD HAVE A PICNIC!

I'M AFRAID WE'LL HAVE TO WAIT UNTIL NEXT SPRING, OLAF!

REALLY? WHY?

WE CAN'T HAVE A PICNIC IN THE SNOW.

OH, THAT'S TRUE...

Manuscript: Tea Orsi; Layout: Emilio Urbano; Cleanup: Nicoletta Baldari; Color: Patrizia Zangrilli

LATER, ANNA TELLS ELSA ABOUT OLAF...

WHAT CAN WE DO?

WELL... WHO SAID THAT PICNICS ARE ONLY FOR OUTDOORS?

TODAY WE'LL HAVE OUR FIRST EVER INDOOR PICNIC!

MY SISTER IS A GENIUS!

WHEN EVERYTHING IS READY...

THREE... TWO...ONE...

CAN I SEE? CAN I SEE? CAN I SEE?

TA-DA!

WELCOME TO YOUR FIRST INDOOR PICNIC, OLAF!

IT'S JUST LIKE SUMMER!

The End

LITTLE INVENTORS

SOMETHING STRANGE IS HAPPENING IN ARENDELLE'S MAIN SQUARE...

YOU LOOK SO BUSY! WHAT ARE YOU DOING?

WE'RE INVENTING!

INVENTING? THAT'S EXCITING.

OH, HI, PRINCESS ANNA! WE'RE SO GLAD TO SEE YOU!

OUCH!

WE'RE CREATING A BICYCLE PINWHEEL. DO YOU LIKE IT?

WONDERFUL! OAKEN WOULD LOVE THIS, TOO.

DO YOU THINK WE COULD BECOME INVENTORS, JUST LIKE HIM?

WE WANT TO SET UP A STALL AND SELL OUR INVENTIONS.

BUT WE DON'T HAVE MANY SUPPLIES TO GET STARTED.

Manuscript: Tea Orsi; Layout and Cleanup: Sara Storino; Color: Dario Calabria

I CAN HELP YOU START YOUR BUSINESS. WAIT FOR ME HERE. I'LL BE RIGHT BACK!

SO...

ANNA, ARE YOU TIDYING UP THE ATTIC?

NOT EXACTLY. THE KIDS NEED RAW MATERIALS TO MAKE INVENTIONS!

THE KIDS? INVENTIONS?

YES! THEY'RE INSPIRED BY OAKEN! THESE OLD TRINKETS WILL HELP THEM START INVENTING.

THAT'S A WONDERFUL IDEA! LET'S HELP THEM!

A FEW DAYS LATER...

YOUR INVENTIONS LOOK GREAT! WHY DO YOU LOOK SO DISAPPOINTED?

NO ONE IS BUYING THEM.

IF YOU WANT TO BE LIKE OAKEN, YOU NEED TO ACT LIKE OAKEN.

COME ONE, COME ALL! THIS SCARF IS SO SOFT AND WILL KEEP YOUR EARS WARM IN THE SNOW!

HUH?! HOW DID YOU COME UP WITH THAT?!

I'D LIKE TO TRY IT ON!

COME ON. GO AHEAD.

HAVE YOU EVER SEEN SUCH A... NON-HUMDRUM DRUM? IT MAKES AN INCREDIBLE RANGE OF DIFFERENT BEATS!

IT'S PERFECT FOR BIRTHDAY PARTIES.

OR TO WAKE UP SOMEONE IN THE MORNING!

CUP OF TEA? WITH OUR TEAPOTCUP YOU WON'T SPILL A DROP!

THAT'S SO SMART! I WON'T STAIN MY EMBROIDERED TABLECLOTH ANYMORE!

SOON...

WE'VE SOLD ALMOST EVERYTHING!

GOODBYE! ENJOY YOUR PURCHASES!

YOU SHOULD SAY **EVERYTHING!** I'LL TAKE WHAT'S LEFT BECAUSE YOU DID A GREAT JOB ON THESE INVENTIONS.

REALLY?!? THANK YOU SO MUCH, PRINCESS ANNA!

LATER...

I SEE YOU ARE DELIVERING MORE STUFF TO THE KIDS?

DELIVERING? OH NO, THESE ARE THEIR CREATIONS! I COULDN'T RESIST!

ISN'T IT FANTASTIC?! NOW OUR OLD ITEMS LOOK COMPLETELY NEW!

YOU'RE RIGHT! HEHEH!

The End

THE SLED RACE

KRISTOFF, OLAF, AND SVEN HAVE A BIG RACE TOMORROW...

THERE IT IS! THAT'S OUR *SLED!*

WOW! IT LOOKS *VERY FAST,* KRISTOFF!

YEAH, IT IS! I CAN'T WAIT TO RACE!

ME TOO! I LOVE SLED RACES!

AND WE'RE GONNA WIN! RIGHT, BUDDY?

I WOULDN'T BE SO SURE OF THAT!

!

?

Manuscript: Valentina Cambi; Layout: Ciro Cangialosi; Pencil: Manuela Razzi; Ink: Roberta Zanotta; Paint: Maria Claudia Di Genova

THE DUKE OF WESELTON!

IN PERSON!

THERE CAN ONLY BE ONE WINNER...

...AND IT'S GOING TO BE *ME.*

YOU'VE STILL GOT TIME TO PULL OUT OF THE RACE!

WE'LL SHOW THAT ARROGANT DUKE WHO'S FASTER!

I'VE NEVER SEEN A SLED BIG LIKE THAT!

UHM... THERE'S SOMETHING STRANGE...

THE SKIS ARE COMPLETELY MADE OF METAL. THEY MUST BE HEAVY, SO THE SLED CAN'T BE VERY FAST... I WONDER WHAT THE DUKE IS UP TO!

WHAT?

I DON'T TRUST HIM EITHER, SVEN!

THE DAY OF THE RACE HAS ARRIVED!

IT'S AN HONOR FOR ARENDELLE TO HOST THE FIRST FJORDS SLED COMPETITION!

GOOD LUCK TO EVERYONE!

MAY THE BEST CONTENDER WIN!

GO, SVEN!

IU-UH!

THE DUKE OF WESELTON IMMEDIATELY TAKES THE LEAD.

NO ONE CAN KEEP UP WITH MY PACE!

BUT SUDDENLY...

?!

WHO'S FASTER NOW?

ME!

A CLOUD!

IT'S NOT A CLOUD, OLAF. IT CAME FROM THE DUKE'S SLED...

...BUT HOW CAN IT BE?

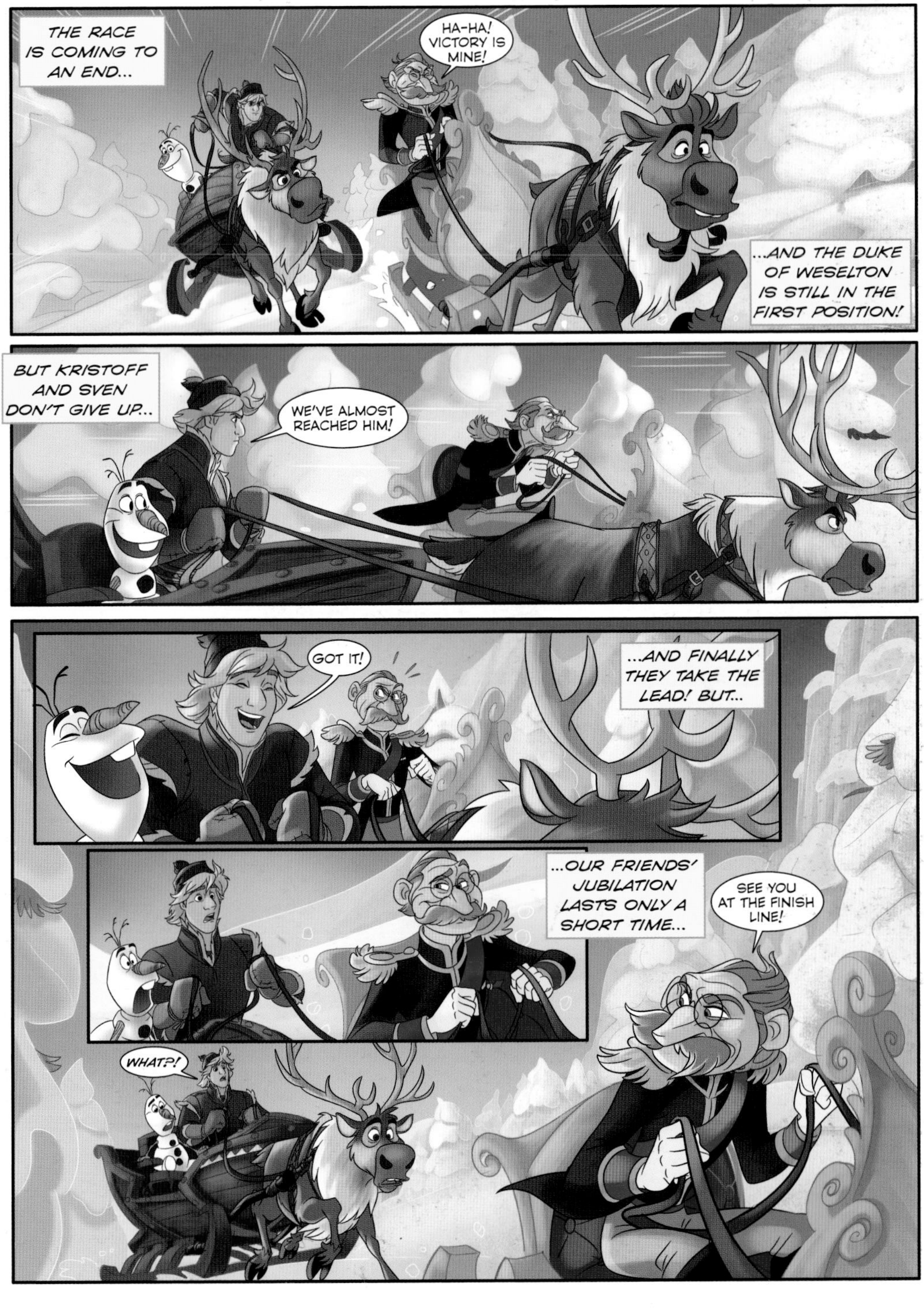
THE RACE IS COMING TO AN END...
HA-HA! VICTORY IS MINE!
...AND THE DUKE OF WESELTON IS STILL IN THE FIRST POSITION!
BUT KRISTOFF AND SVEN DON'T GIVE UP...
WE'VE ALMOST REACHED HIM!
GOT IT!
...AND FINALLY THEY TAKE THE LEAD! BUT...
...OUR FRIENDS' JUBILATION LASTS ONLY A SHORT TIME...
SEE YOU AT THE FINISH LINE!
WHAT?!

KRISTOFF NOTICES SOMETHING WEIRD GOING ON IN THE DUKE'S SLED...

LOOK! THE SKIS SEEM TO HAVE CHANGED COLOR!

BUT IT'S IMPOSSIBLE!

FUN! WHY DON'T WE CHANGE OUR SKIS' COLORS, TOO?

WE CAN'T, OLAF!

THE DUKE MUST BE UP TO SOMETHING...

I WON!

IT'S TIME TO CELEBRATE THE WINNER...

THAT'S FOR YOUR VICTORY, DUKE OF WESELTON!

...BUT SUDDENLY SOMETHING DRAWS OLAF'S ATTENTION!

FRIZZLE

IT'S SO WARM!

STAND BACK, OLAF! IT'S DANGEROUS!

HUH?!

WHAT'S THIS?

THERE'S ONLY ONE WAY TO FIND OUT!

BURNING EMBERS...

...I KNEW SOMETHING WAS SUSPICIOUS...

HEY, WHAT ARE YOU DOING?

WITH THIS BELLOWS AT HIS FEET, HE PUMPED AIR INTO THE SKIS TO KEEP THE EMBERS ALIVE AND SPEED UP WHEN NEEDED!

THE DUKE OF WESELTON DIDN'T EXACTLY PLAY FAIR. HE PUT BURNING EMBERS INSIDE THE SKIS SO THE HEAT COULD MAKE THE SLED GO FASTER ON THE ICE!

IS THIS TRUE, DUKE?

BOO!

PUFF! PUFF!

THAT'S GROUNDS FOR DISQUALIFICATION!

THE WINNERS OF THE RACE ARE KRISTOFF, OLAF, AND SVEN!

BRAVO!

CLAP! CLAP! CLAP!

CLAP! CLAP!

CLAP!

I'VE ALWAYS WANTED A HAT LIKE THIS!

The End

THE TROLL COMPLICATION

Manuscript: Alessandro Ferrari; Layout: Nicoletta Baldari; Cleanup: Rosa La Barbera; Color: Dario Calabria

The End

THE PARA-SNOW

ELSA IS SORTING OUT SOME ACCESSORIES, WHEN...

ELSA, WHAT IS THAT **THING** FOR?

IT'S A PARASOL, OLAF!

PEOPLE OPEN IT TO PROTECT THEMSELVES FROM THE SUNRAYS!

I LIKE IT! DO YOU THINK SNOWMEN CAN USE IT TOO?

WHY NOT? IT MIGHT BE REALLY USEFUL ON THIS **HOT SUMMER** DAY!

AND...

*THIS PARASOL IS AMAZING, BUT IT DIDN'T SEEM SO **HEAVY** BEFORE!

HA HA, FROM NOW ON YOU CAN CALL IT PARASNOW... AND I REALLY LOVE IT!

Manuscript: Tea Orsi; Layout: Emilio Urbano; Cleanup: Miriam Gambino; Color: Dario Calabria

The End

WHERE'S OLAF?

IT'S VERY EARLY IN THE MORNING...

ANNA! IT'S TIME TO WAKE UP!

KNOCK KNOCK

KNOOOCK

KNOOOCK

ANNA, ARE YOU SLEEPING?

NOOO...

I'M COMIN--ZZZ!

OLAF WAITS A BIT LONGER, BUT...

ZZZZZZZ

?!?

Manuscript: Tea Orsi; Layout: Emilio Urbano; Cleanup: Marino Gentile and Nicoletta Baldari; Color: Dario Calabria and Stefania Santi

IN THE END, OLAF DECIDES TO LET ANNA SLEEP.

SHE MUST BE TOO TIRED!

AN HOUR LATER...

HUH?!?

OLAF!

I'M COMING RIGHT AWAY!

OLAF, WHERE DID YOU GO?

IN A JIFFY...

ELSA! HAVE YOU SEEN OLAF? ELSA!?!

SWISH

BUT ANNA COULDN'T FIND ELSA EITHER, SO SHE STARTS SEARCHING BY HERSELF...

OLAF! WHERE ARE YOU HIDING?

OLAAAAF! HUH?!?

KRISTOFF! I CAN'T FIND OLAF ANYWHERE!

AND...

WHAT?!?

HE CAME BY BUT I WAS SO SLEEPY... AND NOW I THINK HE'S LOST!

I'M SURE HE'S NOT LOST! WE'LL FIND HIM!

ANOTHER SEARCH BEGINS...

WE HAVEN'T SEEN HIM!

WHERE COULD HE BE?

MAYBE WITH OAKEN?

HOO HOO, OLAF HASN'T BEEN HERE TODAY!

THANKS ANYWAY, OAKEN!

AND...

MAYBE ELSA KNOWS WHERE OLAF IS.

WHY DIDN'T WE ASK HER BEFORE?!?

WELL... I COULDN'T FIND HER EITHER!

LET'S GO, THEN!

THERE YOU ARE! I'VE BEEN LOOKING FOR YOU EVERYWHERE!

YOU HAVE?

ELSA AND OLAF WANTED ME TO LET YOU KNOW THAT THEY'RE WAITING FOR YOU ON THE NORTH MOUNTAIN!

WHY DIDN'T YOU TELL ME BEFORE?!?

MAYBE BECAUSE YOU WERE SLEEPING?!

OH YEAH, YOU'RE RIGHT.

TO THE NORTH MOUNTAIN, THEN!

READY, SVEN?

OLAF!

ANNA! I'M SO HAPPY YOU'RE HERE!

I'M SORRY I DIDN'T WAKE UP THIS MORNING!

DON'T WORRY, I JUST WANTED YOU TO **COME** WITH US!

I THOUGHT **MARSHMALLOW** MIGHT BE LONELY, AND I WANTED TO VISIT HIM.

BUT YOU WERE STILL SLEEPING, SO WE LEFT YOU A MESSAGE!

GASP!

YAY! NOW WE CAN PLAY **TAG** ALL TOGETHER!

YOU'RE IT, MARSHMALLOW!

THIS IS DEFINITELY THE BEST WAY TO CLEAR UP A MISUNDERSTANDING!

The End

SNOWGIES ON THE ROAD

IT'S A LOVELY, CHILLY DAY IN THE MOUNTAINS...

I CAN'T WAIT TO BE IN MY FAVORITE MOUNTAIN MEADOW!

ME TOO, BUT...

... I WISH **MARSHMALLOW** AND MY LITTLE **BROTHERS** COULD COME WITH US...

WHY NOT? LET'S GO GET THEM!

REALLY?!?

WE'RE STOPPING AT THE ICE PALACE, SVEN!

OUR FRIENDS REACH THEIR FIRST DESTINATION, BUT...

SORRY, MARSHMALLOW! I'M AFRAID MY SLEIGH IS TOO **SMALL** FOR YOU!

OOPS! I THINK HE'LL HAVE TO WALK!

Manuscript: Tea Orsi; Layout: Manuela Razzi; Cleanup: Manuela Razzi; Color: Marco Colletti and Sara Storino

SOON...

WOW! THIS IS SUCH AN EXCITING TRIP!

YEAH, SVEN AND I LOVE CARRYING SO MANY PASSENGERS!

HERE WE ARE! WELCOME TO MY FAVORITE MOUNTAIN MEADOW!

WE'LL HAVE FUN TOGETHER!

WAIT FOR US, LITTLE GUYS!

DON'T GO TOO FAR OR YOU'LL GET LOST!

NOT THE RELAXING TRIP WE HAD IN MIND!

GOT YOU, LITTLE FUGITIVES!

HEY, KRISTOFF! I HAVE AN IDEA!

WHEN IT GETS DARK, WE CAN MAKE ANOTHER TRIP WITH THE BABY TROLLS!

THEY HAVE NEVER BEEN HERE, JUST LIKE MY LITTLE BROTHERS!

ERM...MAYBE TOMORROW, OLAF!

PHEW.

The End

A Guest From Afar

IT'S BREAKFAST TIME AT THE CASTLE!

UH OH!

WHAT'S THE MATTER, ELSA?

PRINCESS ADELAIDE IS COMING TO VISIT TOMORROW. SHE COMES FROM THE FARAWAY KINGDOM OF SELINIA!

CHOMP...THIS IS GREAT!

BUT WHERE SHE LIVES IT'S ALWAYS SUMMER! HOW CAN WE MAKE HER FEEL AT HOME?

!

OOPS! THAT MIGHT BE A PROBLEM!

I KNOW, BUT WE HAVE TO FIND A WAY!

I'M READY!

Manuscript: Tea Orsi; Layout: Emilio Urbano; Cleanup: Veronica Di Lorenzo; Color: Dario Calabria

THE TWO SISTERS ARE LOOKING FOR INFORMATION ABOUT ADELAIDE'S KINGDOM, WHEN...

HEY, WHAT ARE YOU STUDYING?

I'M SO GLAD YOU'RE HERE! MAYBE YOU CAN HELP US!

?!?

?!?

THOSE BOOKS ARE SO BIG!

ONCE KRISTOFF AND OLAF FIND OUT WHAT'S GOING ON...

I CAN'T BELIEVE SHE'S NEVER SEEN THE SNOW!

DON'T WORRY, OLAF. EVERYONE LOVES YOU AND ELSA'S SNOW!

YES, BUT I'M CONCERNED ADELAIDE WILL FEEL TOO COLD HERE!

DOES THAT MEAN SHE HAS NEVER SEEN A SNOWMAN?

WELL... I CAN'T MAKE THE WEATHER WARMER, SO...

WE'LL DECORATE THE CASTLE WITH SOMETHING THAT WILL REMIND ADELAIDE OF SUMMER!

THAT SOUNDS LIKE FUN!

WE CAN HAVE FLOWERS AND FRUITS! AND THE SUMMER SUNSHINE!

ERM...I'M NOT SO SURE WE CAN GET ALL THESE IN ARENDELLE RIGHT NOW, OLAF!

WE'LL FIND SOMETHING. LET'S GO!

GASP!

WHILE ANNA AND KRISTOFF ARE SEARCHING OUTSIDE...

WE'LL MAKE A CAKE WITH STRAWBERRIES AND PEACHES. MAYBE GERDA PRESERVED SOME FROM LAST SUMMER!

IT'S GONNA BE SO COLORFUL!

I'M SORRY, BUT I COULD ONLY FIND NUTS, CHOCOLATE AND APPLES!

WELL... WE'LL MAKE DO WITH THOSE. THANKS, GERDA!

AT SUNSET...

I KNEW WE WOULDN'T FIND ANY SUMMER FLOWERS HERE!

DOWN THERE! I SEE THEM!

BUT CROCUSES ARE WINTER FLOWERS!

I KNOW, SUNFLOWERS WOULD BE BETTER, BUT THEY DON'T GROW IN THIS SEASON.

NEXT MORNING, AFTER A LONG NIGHT OF WORK...

THIS IS BEAUTIFUL ELSA!

IT REALLY FEELS LIKE HOME -- TO ME, ANYWAY!

YES, BUT THERE'S NOTHING THAT FEELS LIKE SUMMER!

COME ON! ARENDELLE IS BEAUTIFUL JUST AS IT IS!

YEAH, OUR WINTER IS AMAZING, ELSA!

I JUST HOPE OUR GUEST LIKES IT AS MUCH AS WE DO...

PRINCESS ADELAIDE FROM THE KINGDOM OF SELINIA IS HERE!

SO EARLY? NOW I HAVE NO TIME TO CHANGE ANYTHING!

CALM DOWN! EVERYTHING'S GONNA BE PERFECT!

YOUR KINGDOM IS WONDERFUL! I LOVE ALL THAT SNOW AND THE COLD WEATHER! IT'S SO REFRESHING!

!

YAY, SHE LIKES THE SNOW!

AND REINDEER ARE LOVELY. I HAD NEVER SEEN THEM BEFORE!

SO YOU DON'T FEEL TOO COLD? AND YOU DON'T MISS THE COLORS OF SUMMER?

NOT AT ALL! I'M USED TO HOT WEATHER, BUT I THINK THAT YOUR WINTER IS KIND OF MAGICAL!

PHEW!

I TOLD YOU ARENDELLE IS BEAUTIFUL AS IT IS!

AND YOU STILL HAVEN'T SEEN THE BEST OF IT!

THIS IS SO MUCH FUN!

YOU'RE RIGHT, ADELAIDE! WINTER IS MAGICAL!

YES! BUT... CAN WE VISIT HER KINGDOM SOMETIME?

The End

SNOW RECORD

Writer: Alessandro Ferrari Artist: Iboix Estudi
Colorist: Charles Pickens Letterer: Patrick Brosseau

The End

WHERE'S EVERYONE?

Manuscript: Tea Orsi; Layout: Zanon Alberto; Cleanup: Veronica Di Lorenzo; Color: Dario Calabria

The End

TROLLS KNOW BEST

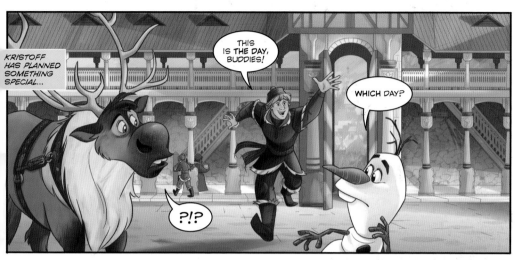

KRISTOFF HAS PLANNED SOMETHING SPECIAL...

THIS IS **THE DAY**, BUDDIES!

WHICH DAY?

?!?

A BIG DAY!

WELL... **EVERY** DAY IS BIG WHEN I'M WITH MY FRIENDS...

YOU'RE RIGHT, BUT TODAY I'M THROWING A **PARTY** FOR ANNA AND ELSA. IN THE TROLL VALLEY!

I LOVE PARTIES!

SHHH, IT'S A SURPRISE!

OOOH! I PROMISE I WON'T SAY ANYTHING!

Manuscript: Tea Orsi; Layout: Emilio Urbano; Cleanup: Veronica Di Lorenzo; Color: Dario Calabria

OLAF AND SVEN OFFER TO HELP KRISTOFF ORGANIZE THE PARTY...

WE'LL ASK KAI AND CAROL FOR ADVICE!

WHAT IF ANNA AND ELSA SEE US?

THEY ARE VISITING MARSHMALLOW; WE HAVE LOTS OF TIME!

KRISTOFF EXPLAINS HIS PLAN TO CAROL AND KAI, AND...

YOU KNOW, I'VE NEVER HOSTED A ROYAL PARTY...

DON'T WORRY!

WE'LL BE HAPPY TO HELP YOU!

THIS BOOK EXPLAINS EVERYTHING ABOUT ROYAL PARTY ETIQUETTE!

GASP! IT'S HUGE!

Royal party Etiquette

DON'T WORRY! WE'LL WRITE DOWN A SHORT LIST FOR YOU!

PHEW! THANKS!

BUT...

ERM... I THOUGHT THEY SAID "SHORT"!

WHEW! THIS WILL BE THE BEST PARTY EVER!

YOU SAID IT! LET'S GET TO WORK!

"FIRST OF ALL, WE NEED FLOWERS..."

MMM, THEY SMELL NICE!

I HOPE THESE WILL BE ENOUGH!

"HERE ARE THE SWEETS... THE CHOCOLATE SWEETS!"

DON'T EVEN THINK ABOUT IT, SVEN!

"AND FINALLY, THE CHINA!"

OHHH!

BE CAREFUL, THEY ARE FRAGILE!

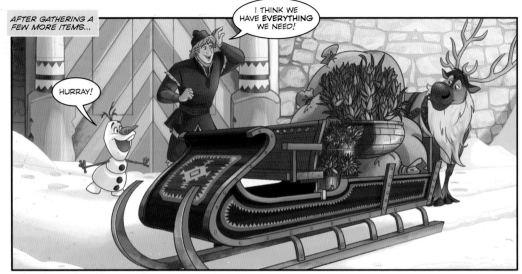

AFTER GATHERING A FEW MORE ITEMS...

I THINK WE HAVE **EVERYTHING** WE NEED!

HURRAY!

NOW IT'S YOUR TURN, BUDDY!

!

TO THE TROLL VALLEY!

AND...

KRISTOFF, WHAT ARE ALL THESE **TRINKETS**?

THEY ARE **NOT TRINKETS**; WE NEED THEM FOR TONIGHT'S ROYAL PARTY!

WE ARE HAVING A **TROLL** PARTY! WE DON'T NEED ALL THAT STUFF!

BUT...ELSA IS A QUEEN AND ANNA'S A PRINCESS! I...

GO AND GET **THEM!** EVERYTHING WILL BE PERFECT!

OKAY...

IT'S TIME TO CELEBRATE!!!

KRISTOFF REACHES THE CASTLE JUST IN TIME FOR ANNA AND ELSA'S RETURN...

WOW! WHAT'S THAT?

DON'T WORRY! JUST CLIMB ABOARD!

HEY! ARE WE HAVING A PARTY?

IS THAT CHOCOLATE?

YES... ERM...NO!

WE'D BETTER GO NOW!

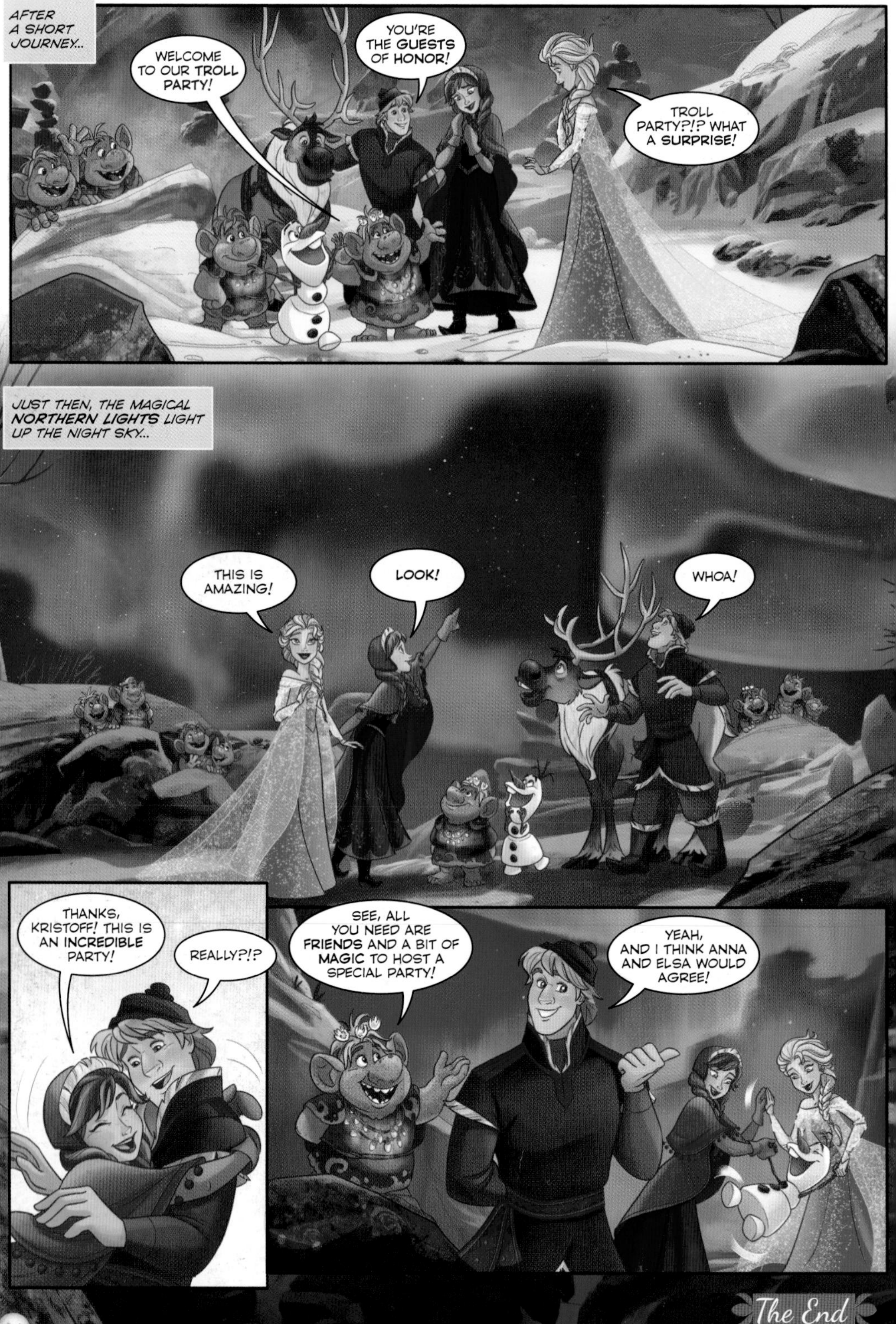
AFTER A SHORT JOURNEY...
WELCOME TO OUR TROLL PARTY!
YOU'RE THE GUESTS OF HONOR!
TROLL PARTY?!? WHAT A SURPRISE!
JUST THEN, THE MAGICAL NORTHERN LIGHTS LIGHT UP THE NIGHT SKY...
THIS IS AMAZING!
LOOK!
WHOA!
THANKS, KRISTOFF! THIS IS AN INCREDIBLE PARTY!
REALLY?!?
SEE, ALL YOU NEED ARE FRIENDS AND A BIT OF MAGIC TO HOST A SPECIAL PARTY!
YEAH, AND I THINK ANNA AND ELSA WOULD AGREE!

The End

THE TOUGH CARROT

Manuscript: Tea Orsi; Layout: Ciro Cangialosi; Cleanup: Sara Storino; Color: MichelAngela World

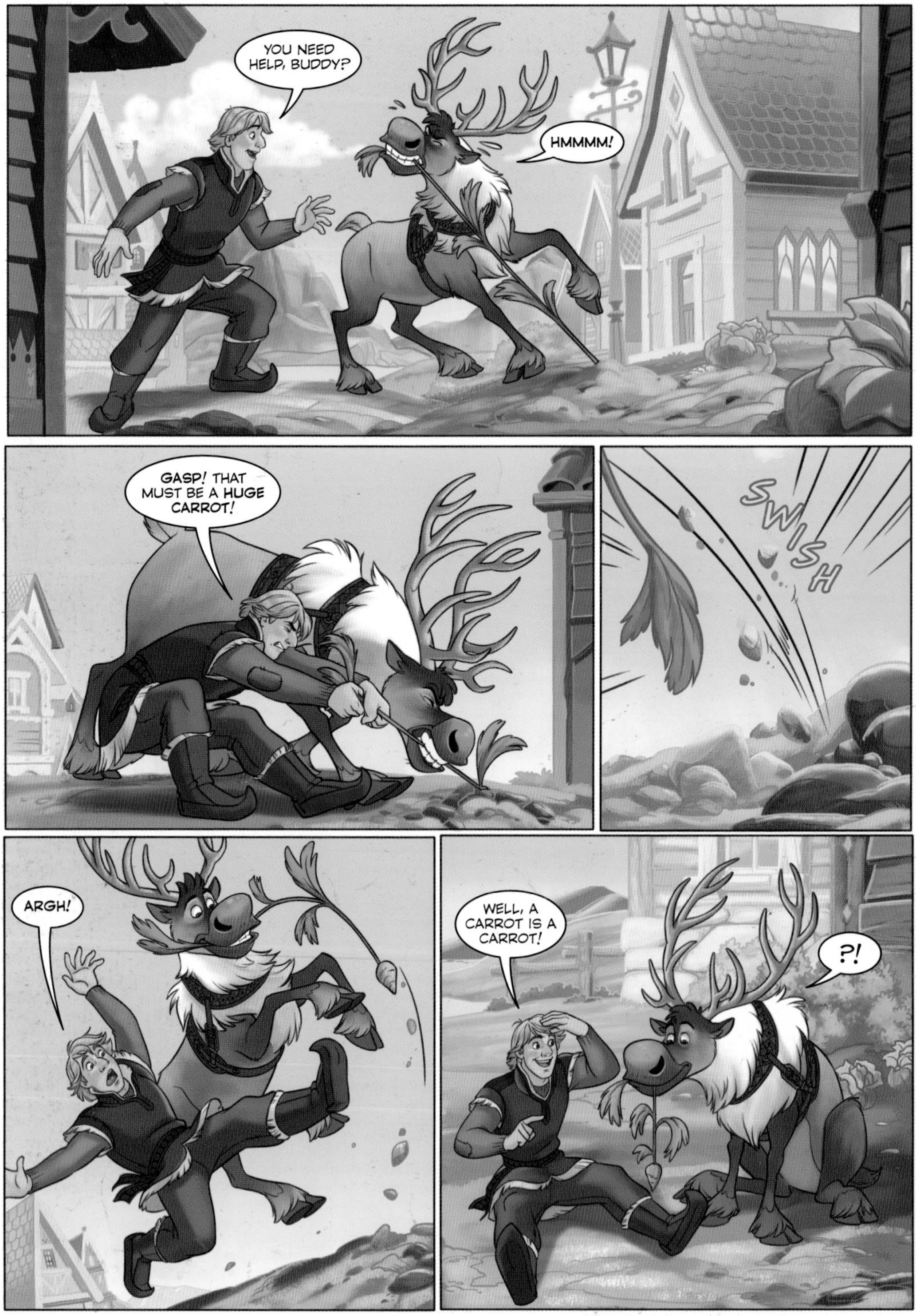
YOU NEED HELP, BUDDY?
HMMMM!
GASP! THAT MUST BE A HUGE CARROT!
SWISH
ARGH!
WELL, A CARROT IS A CARROT!
?!

The End

TRAVEL ARENDELLE

WE'RE GOING HIKING AND I'M SO EXCITED ABOUT IT!

WHAT'S HIKING, ELSA?

IT'S A LONG WALK AFTER A SNUG NIGHT OF CAMPING. READY, ANNA?

ALMOST. I JUST NEED TO SMOTHER THE CAMPFIRE WITH ASHES.

WE DON'T WANT TO LEAVE ANYTHING BURNING WHILE WE HIKE TO WHITE STAG ROCK!

HERE, LET ME HELP.

Script: Georgia Ball; Layouts: Grafimated, Michela Cacciatore; Inks: Michela Cacciatore, Monica Catalano, Veronica Di Lorenzo; Colors: Kat Maximenko, Vita Efremov, Alesya Barsukova, Hanna Chinstova, Anastasiia Belousova, Jackie Lee; Letters: AndWorld Design

I'M CURIOUS...I THOUGHT I KNEW ALL ABOUT OUR KINGDOM'S LANDMARKS, BUT I'VE NEVER HEARD OF WHITE STAG ROCK.

I READ ABOUT IT IN ONE OF MY FAVORITE BOOKS, *PROFESSOR PAULSEN'S GUIDE TO ARENDELLE'S NATURAL WONDERS*.

WHITE STAG ROCK HAS BEEN AROUND FOR CENTURIES. THE BOOK SAYS IT'S VERY EASY TO FIND--ONCE WE GET CLOSE.

WE CAN LEAVE THE CANOE ON THE SHORE--IT'S SECURED. WHITE STAG ROCK IS JUST UP THE HILL.

LET'S TAKE THE RUCKSACK!

LIKE PROFESSOR PAULSEN ALWAYS SAYS: "NEVER LEAVE THE RUCKSACK!"

JUST A LITTLE BIT FARTHER...

...AND IF WE LOOK TO THE RIGHT, WE SHOULD SEE--

...WHITE STAG ROCK!

DOES THAT LOOK LIKE A DEER TO YOU?

MAYBE IF I SQUINT REALLY HARD...

RUMBLE

WHAT'S THAT SOUND? OH, DID SVEN COME ON THE CAMPING TRIP TOO?

RUMBLE RUMBLE RUMBLE RUMBLE

LOTS OF SVENS!

I DON'T THINK THAT'S A REINDEER HERD...

I THINK IT'S--

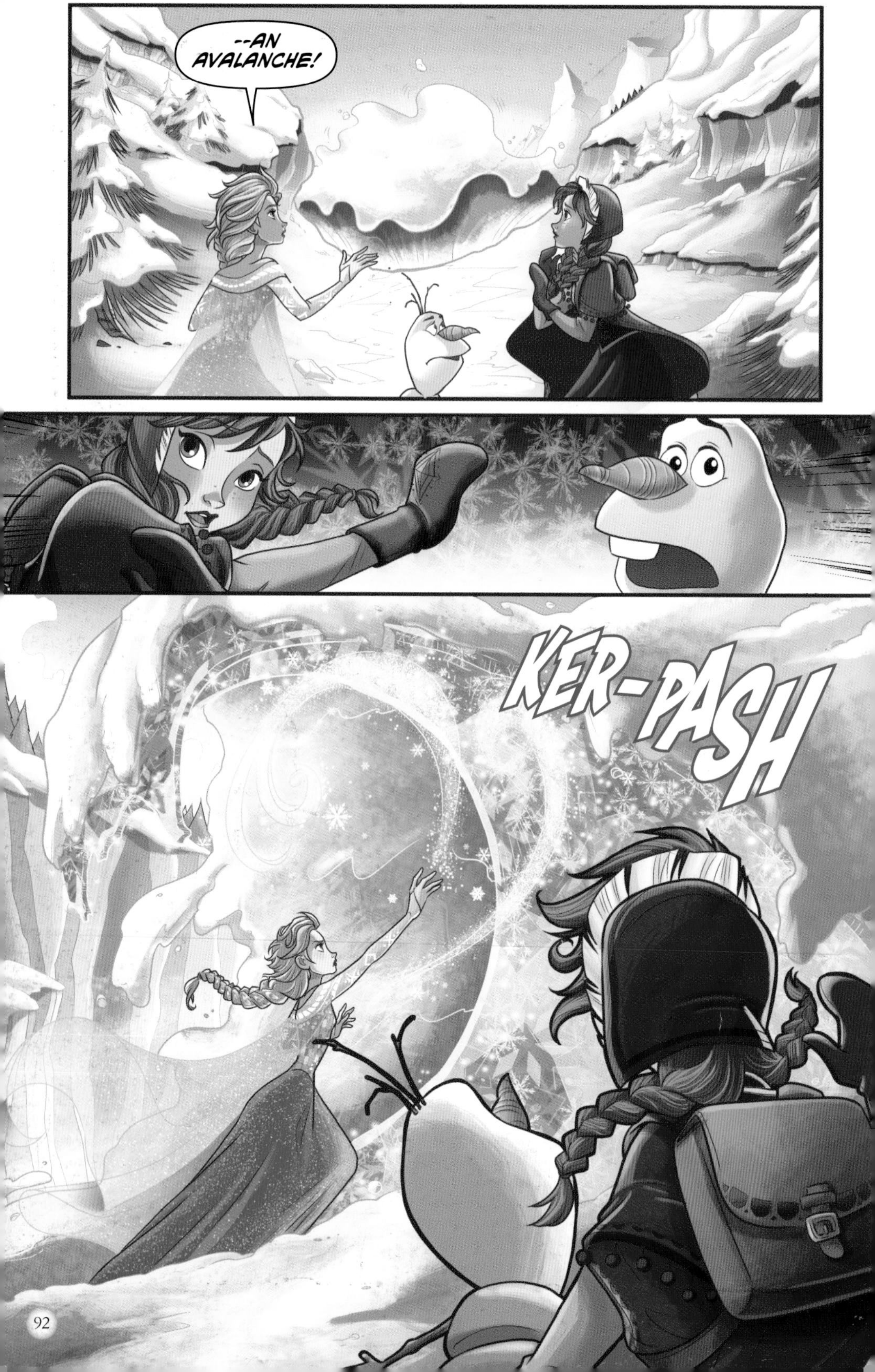
--AN AVALANCHE!
KER-PASH

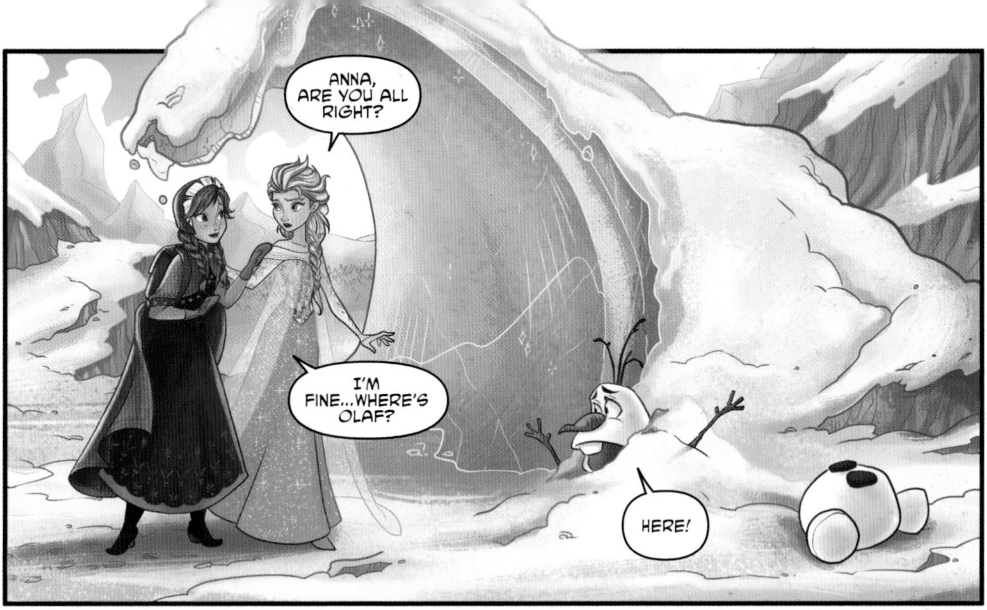
ANNA, ARE YOU ALL RIGHT?
I'M FINE...WHERE'S OLAF?
HERE!

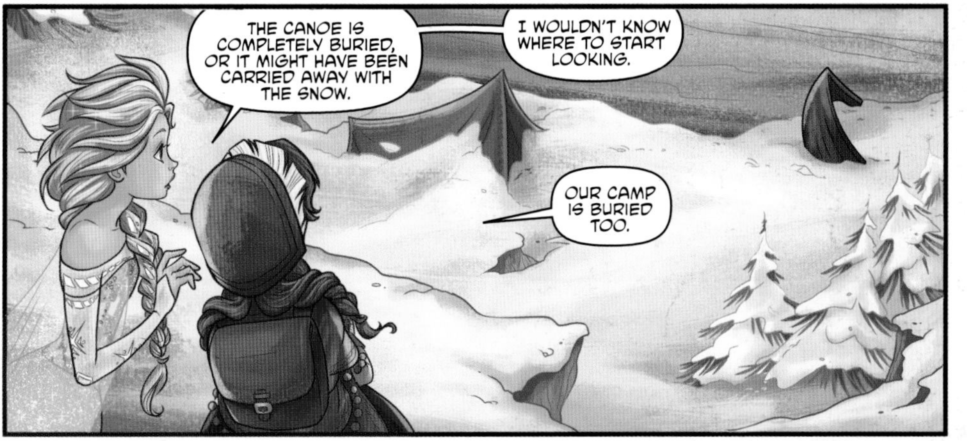
THE CANOE IS COMPLETELY BURIED, OR IT MIGHT HAVE BEEN CARRIED AWAY WITH THE SNOW.
I WOULDN'T KNOW WHERE TO START LOOKING.
OUR CAMP IS BURIED TOO.

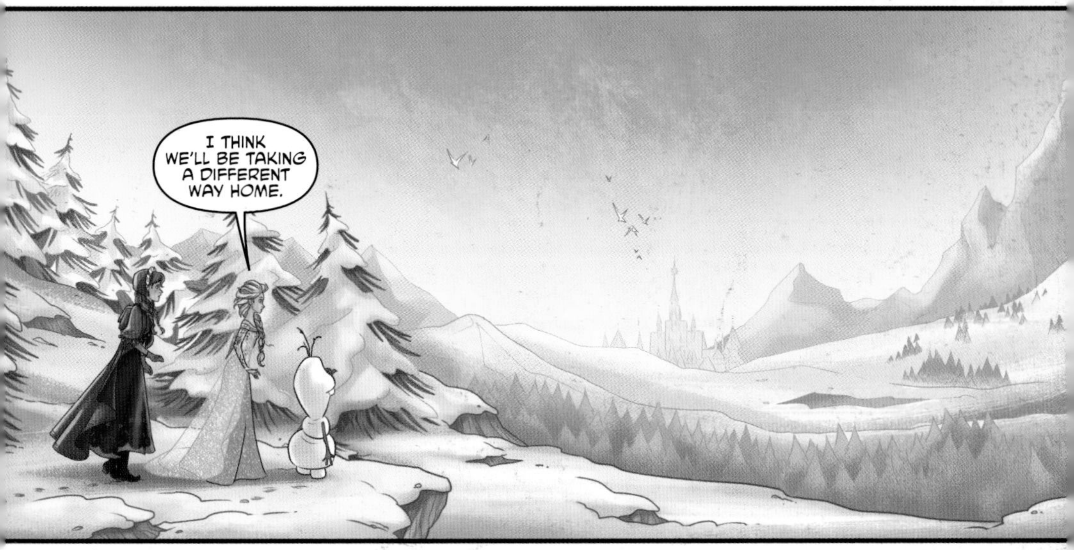
I THINK WE'LL BE TAKING A DIFFERENT WAY HOME.

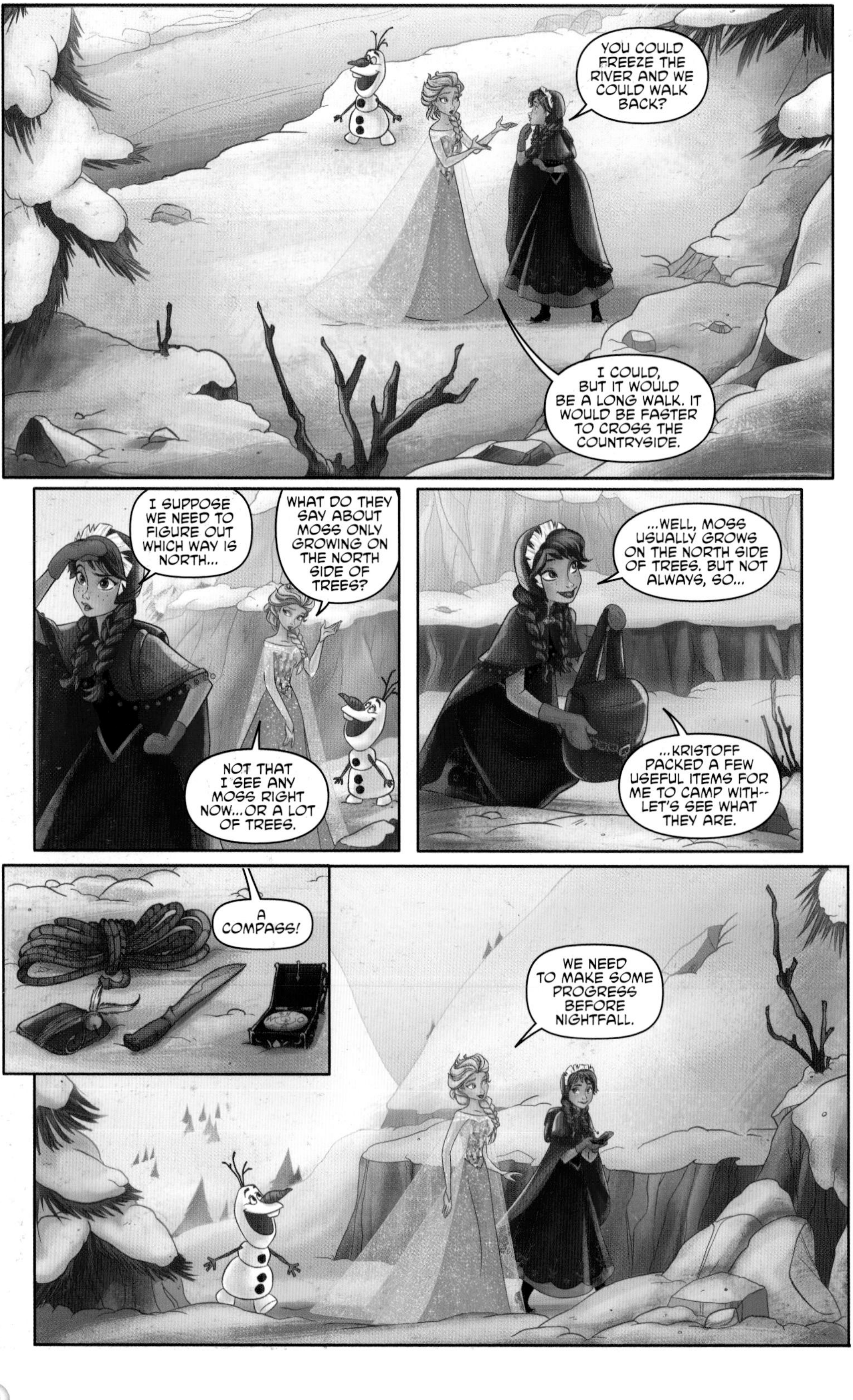
YOU COULD FREEZE THE RIVER AND WE COULD WALK BACK?
I COULD, BUT IT WOULD BE A LONG WALK. IT WOULD BE FASTER TO CROSS THE COUNTRYSIDE.
I SUPPOSE WE NEED TO FIGURE OUT WHICH WAY IS NORTH...
WHAT DO THEY SAY ABOUT MOSS ONLY GROWING ON THE NORTH SIDE OF TREES?
NOT THAT I SEE ANY MOSS RIGHT NOW...OR A LOT OF TREES.
...WELL, MOSS USUALLY GROWS ON THE NORTH SIDE OF TREES. BUT NOT ALWAYS, SO...
...KRISTOFF PACKED A FEW USEFUL ITEMS FOR ME TO CAMP WITH-- LET'S SEE WHAT THEY ARE.
A COMPASS!
WE NEED TO MAKE SOME PROGRESS BEFORE NIGHTFALL.

IT'S GETTING DARK, WE SHOULD STOP FOR THE NIGHT.

THIS LOOKS LIKE A GOOD SPOT!

THE STARS ARE OUT. I HEARD ONCE THAT EXPLORERS USED THEM TO FIND THEIR WAY.

IS THAT THE CHARIOT CONSTELLATION?

THE NORTH STAR SHOULD BE FIVE TIMES THE DISTANCE BETWEEN THE TWO POINTER STARS IN THE DIRECTION THEY'RE POINTING TO...

I DON'T REMEMBER MY ASTRONOMY QUITE SO WELL...

...REMEMBER HOW FATHER KNEW THE NAMES OF ALL THE CONSTELLATIONS?

YES!

I WISH WE COULD HAVE SPENT MORE TIME LOOKING AT THE STARS TOGETHER AS KIDS, BUT AT LEAST WE HAVE EACH OTHER TO RELY ON NOW.

I AGREE!

YOU MUST BE GETTING COLD, ANNA. OLAF AND I WILL BE OKAY...

...BUT THIS SHOULD KEEP YOU WARM!

OOH, HOW COZY!

ICE CAN KEEP YOU *WARM?*

IT WILL IF WE BUILD A FIRE.

OOO! I WANT TO HELP BUILD THE FIRE!

OKAY OLAF... JUST DON'T GET TOO CLOSE!

I COULD SLEEP IN ONE OF THESE ANY TIME.

ARENDELLE LOOKS MUCH CLOSER NOW. I THINK WE'LL GET THERE BY THIS AFTERNOON.

THAT'S GOOD NEWS, BUT I AM A LITTLE THIRSTY.

I DON'T SEE ANY WATER, JUST ALL OF THIS SNOW EVERYWHERE...

THERE'S *FROZEN* WATER ALL AROUND US, OLAF.

ANNA, WAIT! THE SNOW IS TOO COLD, YOU'LL FREEZE!

IT'S OKAY, I'LL SHOW YOU WHAT I'M GOING TO DO...

...IF I KEEP THE CONTAINER INSIDE MY CLOTHES, MY BODY HEAT WILL MELT THE SNOW.

WHEN THE WATER GETS WARM ENOUGH I'LL DRINK IT. THAT'S ANOTHER ONE OF PROFESSOR PAULSEN'S HELPFUL TIPS!

MAY I BORROW THAT BOOK SOMETIME?

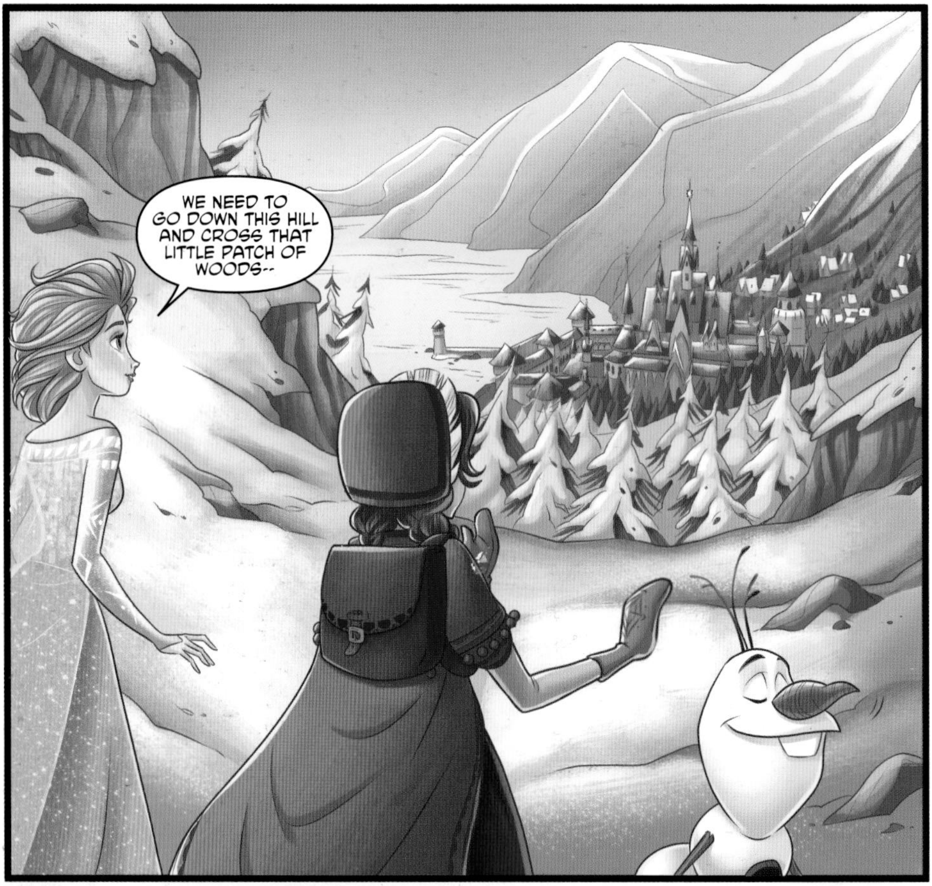
WE NEED TO GO DOWN THIS HILL AND CROSS THAT LITTLE PATCH OF WOODS--

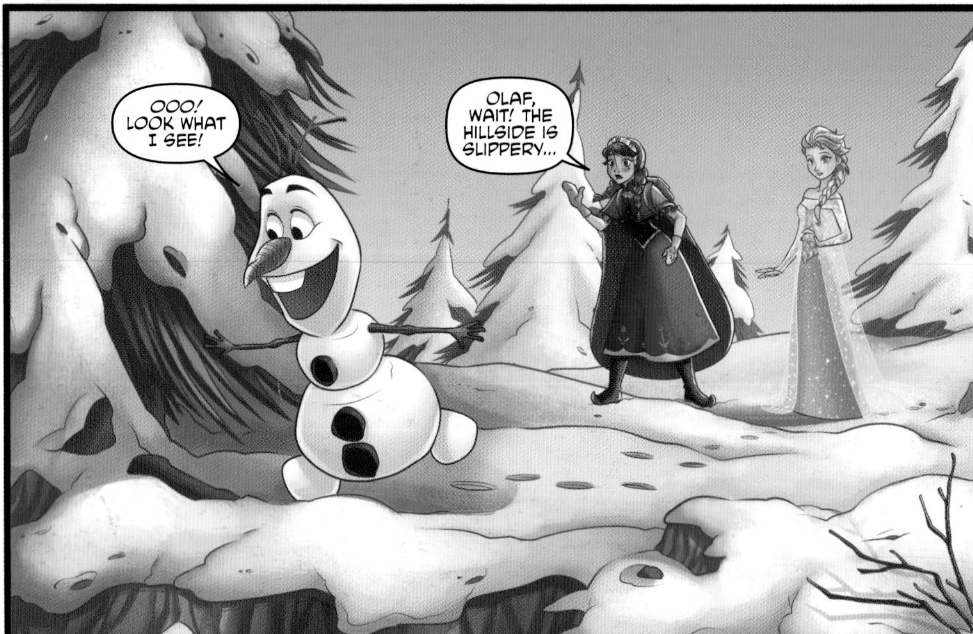
OOO! LOOK WHAT I SEE!
OLAF, WAIT! THE HILLSIDE IS SLIPPERY...

OLAF!!!

WE WERE AFRAID YOU'D FALLEN OFF.

I DIDN'T FALL. I SAW A BERRY BUSH!

I GUESS THE BIRDS MISSED THIS LITTLE BUNCH OF BERRIES! JUST LOOKING AT IT REMINDS ME OF SUMMER.

I LOVE SUMMER, SO I LOVE BLACKBERRIES!

THEN FROM NOW ON YOU'LL SEE BLACKBERRIES ALL YEAR LONG.

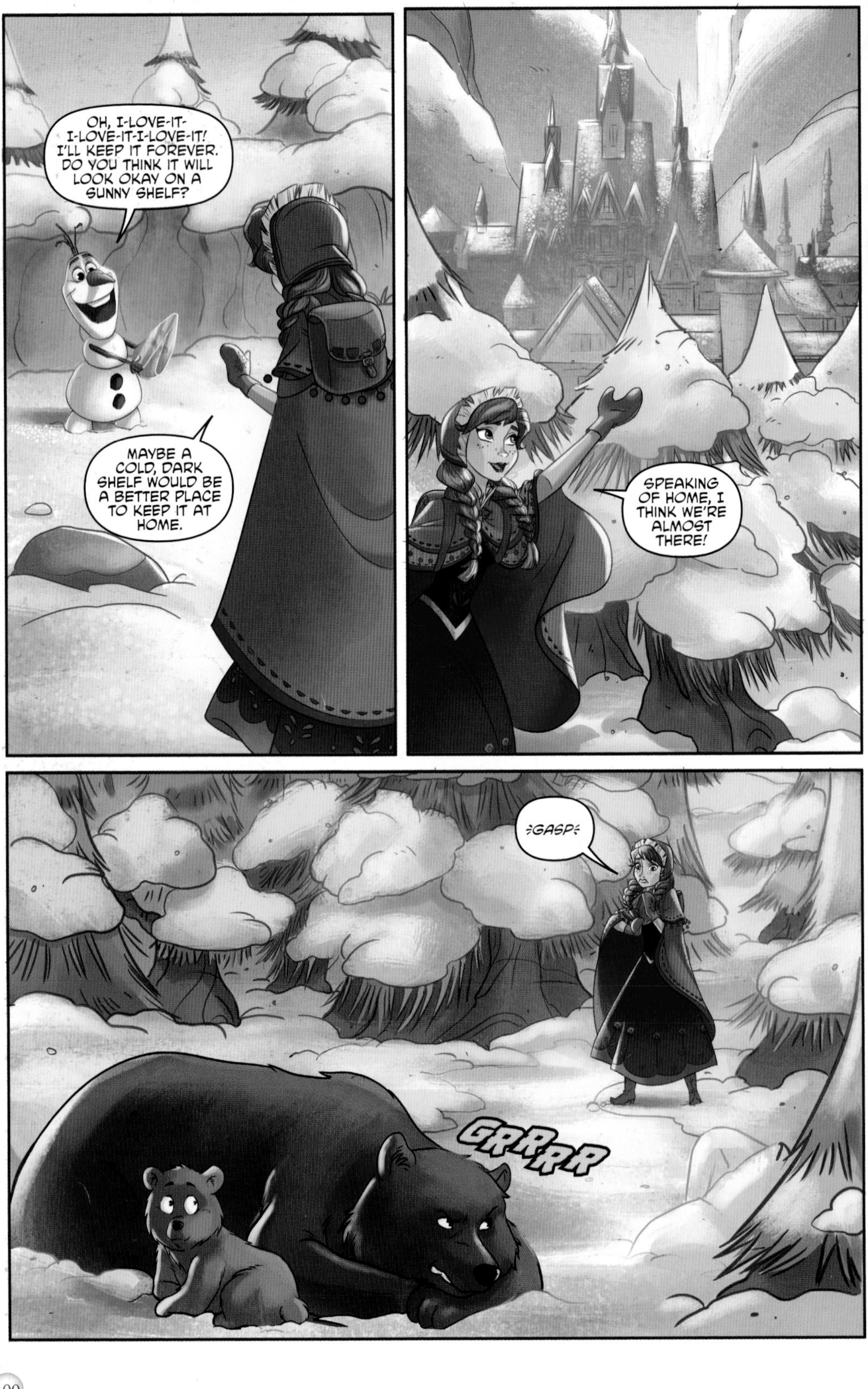
OH, I-LOVE-IT-I-LOVE-IT-I-LOVE-IT! I'LL KEEP IT FOREVER. DO YOU THINK IT WILL LOOK OKAY ON A SUNNY SHELF?
MAYBE A COLD, DARK SHELF WOULD BE A BETTER PLACE TO KEEP IT AT HOME.
SPEAKING OF HOME, I THINK WE'RE ALMOST THERE!
GASP
GRRRR

ROOOAAARRR!

ANNA! THIS WAY!

SHOOOOOO

WHERE'S OLAF?

OLAF! NO!

THAT MOTHER BEAR IS TRYING TO PROTECT HER CUB. WE HAVE TO STOP HIM BEFORE HE GETS HURT!

STAND BACK, I'LL BREAK THE ICE.

KAPASH

OLAF!

YOU'RE NOT MISSING ANY PIECES?

NO. WHY?

WHERE DID THE BEARS GO?

THEY WENT AWAY.

THEY DID? WHY?

WELL, I REMEMBERED THAT KRISTOFF SAID THAT BEARS LIKE BLACKBERRIES...

"...I GAVE MY GLOBE TO THE CUB. THE MOTHER BEAR WAS REALLY NICE AFTER THAT."

THAT WAS VERY KIND OF YOU, OLAF. I KNOW YOUR NEW GLOBE MEANT A LOT TO YOU.

THAT'S OKAY. I LIKE MAKING NEW FRIENDS!

WHAT A STORY! WE WERE ABOUT TO ORGANIZE A SEARCH PARTY FOR YOU--I'M JUST GLAD YOU'RE ALL HOME SAFE.

SAFE AND SOUND--THANKS TO ANNA'S WILDERNESS KNOW-HOW.

AND ELSA'S QUICK THINKING.

BUT MOST OF ALL--

--THANKS TO OLAF'S SELFLESS HEART.

The End

Snow-Breather

ARENDELLE CASTLE. A *FAIR* IS COMING IN A FEW DAYS AND EVERYONE IS GETTING READY...

ANNA! I FOUND IT! I KNOW WHAT I WANT TO DO AT THE FAIR...

...I WILL BE A FIRE-BREATHER!

!

"IT'LL BE SO GREAT TO SHOOT FIRE FOR THE PEOPLE OF ARENDELLE. IT'LL BE A SHOW LIKE NO ONE HAS EVER SEEN BEFORE!"

WELL... I THINK YOU'D BE GREAT, NATURALLY...

ME TOO, ANNA.

...BUT MAYBE THINGS WON'T GO EXACTLY AS YOU IMAGINE.

WHY?

WELL... I THINK...

I KNOW YOU CAN DO IT, OLAF!

ELSA!

SERIOUSLY? I MEAN... OF COURSE... BUT HOW?

Manuscript: Alessandro Ferrari; Layout: Nicoletta Baldari; Cleanup: Nicoletta Baldari; Color: Dario Calabria

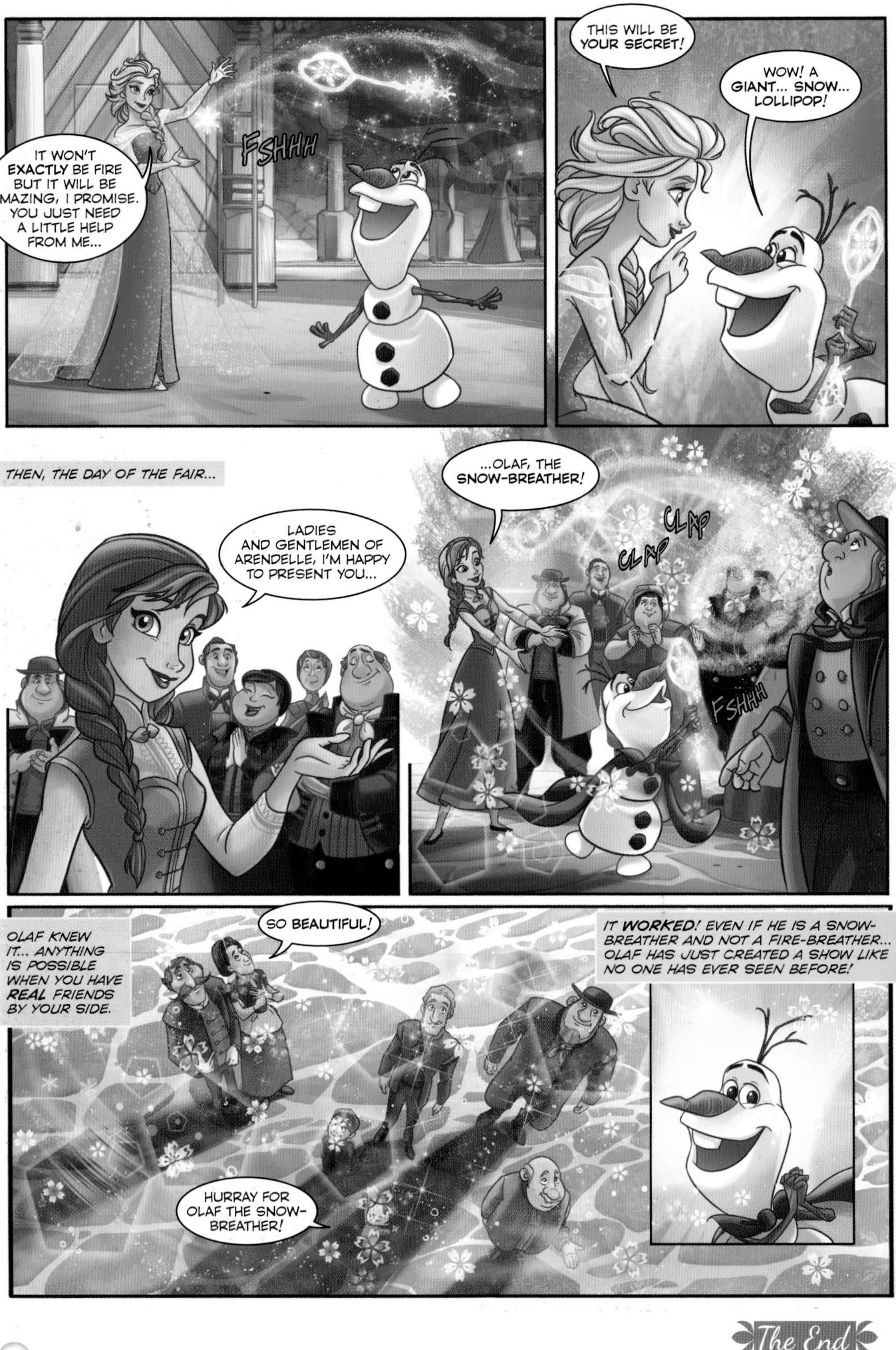
IT WON'T **EXACTLY** BE FIRE BUT IT WILL BE AMAZING, I PROMISE. YOU JUST NEED A LITTLE HELP FROM ME...
FSHHH
THIS WILL BE YOUR SECRET!
WOW! A GIANT... SNOW... LOLLIPOP!
THEN, THE DAY OF THE FAIR...
LADIES AND GENTLEMEN OF ARENDELLE, I'M HAPPY TO PRESENT YOU...
...OLAF, THE **SNOW-BREATHER!**
CLAP
CLAP
FSHHH
*OLAF KNEW IT... ANYTHING IS POSSIBLE WHEN YOU HAVE **REAL** FRIENDS BY YOUR SIDE.*
SO **BEAUTIFUL!**
*IT **WORKED!** EVEN IF HE IS A SNOW-BREATHER AND NOT A FIRE-BREATHER... OLAF HAS JUST CREATED A SHOW LIKE NO ONE HAS EVER SEEN BEFORE!*
HURRAY FOR OLAF THE SNOW-BREATHER!
The End

A Funny Show

Manuscript: Tea Orsi; Layout and Cleanup: Nicoletta Baldari; Color: Dario Calabria

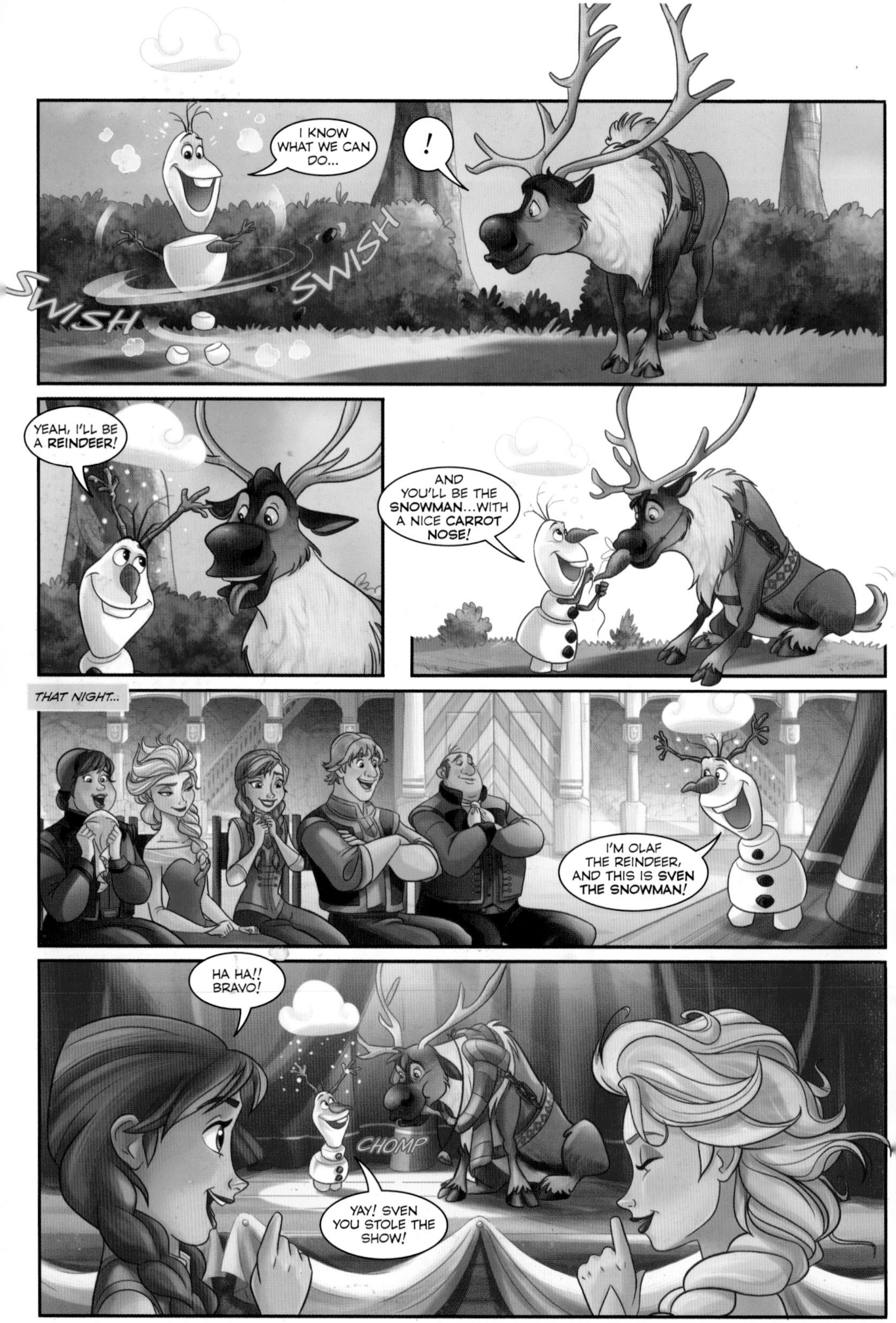
I KNOW WHAT WE CAN DO...
!
SWISH
SWISH
YEAH, I'LL BE A REINDEER!
AND YOU'LL BE THE SNOWMAN...WITH A NICE CARROT NOSE!
THAT NIGHT...
I'M OLAF THE REINDEER, AND THIS IS SVEN THE SNOWMAN!
HA HA!! BRAVO!
CHOMP
YAY! SVEN YOU STOLE THE SHOW!

The End

LITTLE EXPLORERS

ANNA HAS A COLD...

OH, I REALLY WANTED TO GO OUT TODA-A-A-AATCHOO!

COME ON, ANNA! YOU'LL BE BETTER SOON!

I KNOW! SNIFF...BUT THIS IS SO BORING...

LET'S SEE IF THIS WILL MAKE YOU CHANGE YOUR MIND!

GASP! THAT WAS ONE OF OUR FAVORITE BOOKS!

I KNEW YOU WOULD REMEMBER IT!

OF COURSE I DO! IT'S THE STORY OF THE TWO KIDS WHO GOT LOST AND...

LIVED A FANTASTIC ADVENTURE IN AN UNEXPLORED LAND!

Manuscript: Tea Orsi; Layout: Alberto Zanon; Cleanup: Letizia Algeri; Color: Dario Calabria

WHAT IS AN UNEXPLORED LAND, ANNA?

OH, HI OLAF!

IT'S A PLACE NO ONE HAS GOTTEN TO KNOW YET.

REALLY?!? TELL ME **MORE** ABOUT THIS STORY!

ATCHOO!

WE'LL **READ** IT TOGETHER!

YES, WHEN WE WERE LITTLE WE LOVED IT SO MUCH THAT ONCE WE TRIED TO **IMITATE** IT!

"IT WAS A SUNNY AFTERNOON AND OUR MOTHER WAS READING THE BOOK OUT LOUD FOR US..."

SO THE KIDS FOUND THEIR WAY HOME, AND THEY LOOKED FORWARD TO TELLING EVERYONE ABOUT...

...THEIR AMAZING ADVENTURE!

"AND AFTER THE STORY, WE COULDN'T WAIT TO PLAY..."

DON'T GO TOO FAR, GIRLS!

WE'RE GOING TO EXPLORE THE WOODS, MOMMY!

LET'S GO, ELSA! I WANT TO FIND A NEW LAND, LIKE THE KIDS IN THE BOOK!

GOOD IDEA, ANNA!

WOW! DID YOU FIND THE UNKNOWN LAND?

WELL, WE PRETENDED IT WAS IN THE WOODS!

WE DIDN'T KNOW IT THAT WELL, SO IT WAS KIND OF UNEXPLORED FOR US!

"SO WE STARTED LOOKING AROUND..."

THESE MUST BE YUMMYLICIOUS BERRIES...

HMMM... THEY DON'T LOOK LIKE THE ONES IN THE BOOK. WHAT IF THEY'RE NOT EDIBLE?

IT'S NOT FAIR! IN THE BOOK ALL THE BERRIES WERE DELICIOUS!

"BUT WE KEPT HAVING FUN ANYWAY..."

A MONSTER MUST HAVE PASSED THROUGH HERE!

LET'S FOLLOW ITS FOOTPRINTS!

"AND WE DIDN'T NOTICE THAT THE TIME WAS PASSING REALLY FAST..."

HA HA!

KEEP DANCING!

"UNTIL..."

GASP! IT'S LATE! WE HAVE TO GO BACK!

"BUT..."

THAT'S OKAY! WE'LL STAY HERE AND SLEEP UNDER THE **STARS** LIKE REAL EXPLORERS!

WHERE ARE WE?!? ANNA, I DON'T REMEMBER WHERE WE CAME FROM!

ANNA, I THINK WE ARE LOST!

THE KIDS IN THE BOOK GOT LOST TOO!

BUT THEY CLIMBED THE HIGH MOUNTAIN AND SAW THEIR HOME FROM UP THERE!

THERE IS NO MOUNTAIN HERE, ANNA...

WAIT A MINUTE, MAYBE...

I CAN TRY TO MAKE IT!

YOU'RE RIGHT! DO THE MAGIC, ELSA!

WHAT DID YOU MAKE ELSA?

IT WAS...

"...SOMETHING THAT LOOKED LIKE A MOUNTAIN...!"

"IT TURNED OUT THAT OUR UNEXPLORED LAND WAS JUST A FEW STEPS AWAY FROM OUR PARENTS."

LOOK! THEY ARE DOWN THERE!

I CAN'T BELIEVE IT!

MAYBE WE WERE NOT SO LOST AS WE THOUGHT!

NOW, LET'S READ THE ORIGINAL STORY!

I THINK I'M FEELING MUCH BETTER!

LET'S PLAN A NEW ADVENTURE FOR TOMORROW!

CAN I COME TOO?

SURE!

AAAAATCHOOOOO!

WELL, MAYBE WE'LL GO THE DAY AFTER TOMORROW!

The End

THE PERFECT NOSE

ELSA, ANNA AND OLAF HAVE JUST MADE A SNOWMAN TOGETHER...

NOW WE JUST NEED A NICE CARROT NOSE!

ERM...I'M NOT SURE THERE ARE ANY LEFT...

SVEN?!?

CHOMP

SILLY SVEN!

ONE ICE CARROT, COMING UP!

WOW!

OOPS, SVEN LIKES IT TOO, DON'T YA BUDDY?

BUT, THE ICE CARROT IS TOO COLD AND...

UH-OH! SVEN IS STUCK!

POOR SVEN!

The End

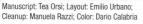

Manuscript: Tea Orsi; Layout: Emilio Urbano; Cleanup: Manuela Razzi; Color: Dario Calabria

QUESTION OF BALANCE

OLAF WANTS TO PLAY WITH A NEW SEE-SAW AND ANNA JOINS HIM.

OOPS, WE'RE STUCK!

IF ONLY SNOW WAS HEAVIER...

I KNOW WHAT TO DO

OLAF COMES BACK WITH A LOT OF NEW "BUTTONS", BUT...

OH NO!

I'M SORRY, BUT YOU'RE STILL LIGHTER THAN ME.

DON'T WORRY, I'VE GOT AN IDEA!

AND SOON...

WELL... NOW WE'RE STUCK IN THE OPPOSITE WAY!

WOW THAT WAS FUN!

Manuscript: Tea Orsi; Layout: Marino Gentile; Cleanup: Nicoletta Baldari; Paint: Dario Calabria

The End

A Gift For Marshmallow

Manuscript: Tea Orsi; Layout: Emilio Urbano; Cleanup: Nicoletta Baldari; Color: Stefania Santi

KRISTOFF EXPLAINS HIS PLAN AND LATER, AT THE ICE PALACE...

ARE YOU SURE MARSHMALLOW IS ENJOYING HIS GIFT?

OF COURSE!

BABYSITTING THESE LITTLE ONES IS A TOUGH JOB!

MAYBE, BUT...

...IT'S SO MUCH FUN!

I'M SURE MARSHMALLOW AGREES, BUT...

"...IT'S SOMETIMES NICE TO HAVE A LITTLE TIME FOR YOURSELF!"

AAAH!

The End

THE MIDWINTER RIDE

SOME IMPORTANT GUESTS ARE IN ARENDELLE FOR A SPECIAL MIDWINTER CELEBRATION...

WHAT ARE WE WAITING FOR? I'M FREEZING!

WHEN KRISTOFF COMES WE'LL SET OFF ON OUR NIGHT RIDE, DUKE.

I KNEW I SHOULDN'T HAVE COME HERE WITH YOU!

WHERE'S KRISTOFF?

HE SHOULD ALREADY BE HERE WITH THE LANTERNS.

I CAN'T WAIT TO SHOW THEM TO OUR GUESTS! OAKEN MADE THEM FOR US.

ELDORA

CHATO

ARENDELLE

TIKAANI

WESELTON

THEY REPRESENT OUR DIFFERENT KINGDOMS, AND...

Original story by Erica David; Adapted by Tea Orsi;
Layout & Clean: Marino Gentile; Ink & Color: MichelAngela World

119

"... WE WILL HANG THEM TOGETHER TO LIGHT UP OUR WAY!"

"A LANTERN-LIT RIDE! WHAT A GREAT WAY TO CELEBRATE THE FRIENDSHIP AMONG OUR KINGDOMS!"

YES, BUT I'M AFRAID SOMEONE WON'T WAIT ANY LONGER...

JUST THEN...

TLOT TLOT TLOT

SVEN!?

WHAT HAPPENED?

IS THAT REINDEER HURT?

I DON'T THINK SO...

TUMP TUMP

120

WAIT... WHERE IS KRISTOFF? IS HE IN TROUBLE?

!

TAKE ME TO HIM, SVEN!

ANNA! WAIT!

TLOT TLOT TLOT

WE CAN'T LET THEM GO ON THEIR OWN!

LET'S FOLLOW THEM!

WE'LL ALL COME WITH YOU!

YES!

DUKE, I'M AFRAID WE HAVE TO DELAY THE RIDE, BUT...

I'M COMING, TOO. I'VE WAITED LONG ENOUGH!

121

MEANWHILE, ANNA AND SVEN HAVE REACHED THE WOODS.

KRISTOFF!? WHERE ARE YOU?

ANNA! WE'RE HERE!

KRISTOFF!

ARE YOU OKAY? WHAT HAPPENED?

WE'RE STUCK!

?!

SWOOSH

TLOT TLOT

IT SEEMS A WHOLE **RESCUE TEAM** HEARD YOUR CALL!

HOW CAN WE HELP?

IS ANYONE HURT?

THIS WOODSMAN HAS A BROKEN ANKLE.

THE SNOW WAS SO DEEP THAT I LOST MY FOOTING...

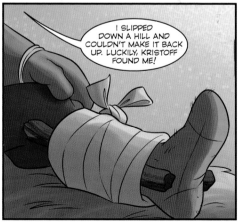

I SLIPPED DOWN A HILL AND COULDN'T MAKE IT BACK UP. LUCKILY, KRISTOFF FOUND ME!

BUT THAT BRANCH FELL FROM THE TREE AND BLOCKED US, SO I SENT SVEN TO LOOK FOR HELP!

OH NO! YOUR SLEIGH!

I HAVE AN IDEA!

IF WE JOIN FORCES, WE CAN MOVE THE BRANCH!

WE HAVE TO PULL THAT HUGE THING?! NOT THAT I'M NOT STRONG ENOUGH, BUT...

HEE HAW NEEEEIGH WOOF WOOF

DON'T WORRY, DUKE. I THINK WE'VE GOT SOME **EXTRA** HELP...

I KNEW WE COULD ALWAYS COUNT ON YOU, SVEN!

!

EVERYONE DOES THEIR PART, AND...

WE ARE READY!

OKAY!

TRRRR

COME ON, FRIENDS! I KNOW WE CAN DO IT!

WE DID IT!

AMAZING!

WROOOSH

NOW WE'LL GO HOME AND TAKE CARE OF YOUR ANKLE!

THANK YOU! YOU SAVED US!

BUT...

I KNEW IT... YOUR **PRESENTS** ARE DAMAGED.

DON'T WORRY, KRISTOFF. WE'RE GLAD YOU'RE SAFE.

PRESENTS? LANTERNS? WERE THEY FOR US?

YES, ANNA AND I WANTED ALL OF US TO HAVE IDENTICAL LANTERNS...

THEY **REPRESENTED** THE **UNITY** OF OUR KINGDOMS. I PROMISE WE'LL HAVE THEM READY FOR THE NEXT WINTER CELEBRATION AND...

DON'T WORRY, THE MEMORY OF THIS TEAM RESCUE IS THE BEST KEEPSAKE FOR US ALL!

YES, ONLY GOOD FRIENDS WORK TOGETHER AS WE JUST DID!

I CAN'T HELP BUT AGREE. THIS TIME.

SEE? EVEN MISADVENTURES CAN TURN INTO GREAT MEMORIES!

The End

THE NEW GLOVES

ANNA HAS JUST KNITTED A NEW PAIR OF MITTENS...

TA-DAH! DO YOU LIKE THEM?

THEY ARE LOVELY!

AND THEY LOOK EXACTLY LIKE SVEN!

YEAH, I KNOW...

AND I ALSO MADE THESE!

WOW! THEY LOOK LIKE OLAF!

THAT'S WHY I LOVE BOTH PAIRS...AND I DON'T KNOW WHICH ONE TO WEAR!

WELL, MAYBE I KNOW WHAT WE CAN DO...

ELSA TELLS ANNA ABOUT HER IDEA, AND...

YOU ARE THE BEST SISTER EVER, ELSA!

YOUR MITTENS ARE AMAZING!

Manuscript: Tea Orsi; Layout: Nicoletta Baldari; Color: Dario Calabria

The End

A Hard Decision

TODAY ELSA HAS A LOT OF THINGS TO DO...

HELLO, ELSA!

HI, OLAF!

A WHILE LATER...

HELLO, ELSA!

HUH?! YOU ARE HERE TOO!

THEN...

OLAF?!?

HI, ELSA!

YOU ARE REALLY BUSY THIS MORNING. I'VE SEEN YOU IN EVERY ROOM!

ANNA TOLD ME THAT IT'S NICE TO SPEND TIME IN YOUR FAVORITE ROOM...

... BUT I LOVE ALL THE ROOMS IN THE CASTLE, SO...

I'M JUST TRYING TO SPEND SOM TIME IN EAC OF THEM!

Manuscript: Tea Orsi; Layout: Alberto Zanon; Cleanup: Rosa La Barbera; Color: Ekaterina Makimenko

The End

A Huge Help

ELSA AND FRIENDS HAVE JUST VISITED THE ICE PALACE...

FASTER, SVEN!

THERE'S A BIG BUNCH OF **CARROTS** WAITING FOR YOU AT THE CASTLE!

WOOSH

AND HOT **CHOCOLATE** FOR THE REST OF US!

HUH? DID YOU HEAR THAT?

HOOOOO

HOOOOO

IT'S COMING FROM THAT LEDGE!

IT SOUNDS LIKE AN ANIMAL IN DANGER!

AND...

IT'S A SLED DOG! HOW DID HE END UP DOWN THERE?

I DON'T KNOW BUT WE HAVE TO **RESCUE** HIM!

HELLO-O-O! I CAN'T WAIT TO GIVE YOU A WARM HUG!

Manuscript: Tea Orsi; Layout: Alberto Zanon; Cleanup: Caterina Giorgetti; Color: MichelAngela World

I WILL GO DOWN THERE AND YOU'LL **PULL** US UP!

MAYBE WE WON'T NEED TO DO THAT, ANNA!

?!?

IT'S MARSHMALLOW! HE MUST HAVE HEARD THE DOG HOWLING!

HE WANTS TO **HUG** HIM TOO!

THANK YOU, MARSHMALLOW!

YOU SAVED OUR NEW FRIEND!

!?!

YOU DESERVE THAT VERY SPECIAL "THANK YOU"!

SLURP

The End

A Snowy Night

HOPEFULLY THIS WILL BE A GOOD NIGHT TO SEE THE NORTHERN LIGHTS...

I CAN'T WAIT TO EAT GERDA'S SANDWICHES. THIS HIKE MADE ME SO HUNGRY!

HOW DO YOU FEEL WHEN YOU'RE HUNGRY, ANNA?

YOU FEEL A BIT WEAK AND YOUR STOMACH GRUMBLES! LIKE THIS...

HERE WE ARE!

HUH?!?

BROOOP

WE CAN FINALLY ENJOY OUR PICNIC AND WATCH THE LIGHTS!

YEAH, BUT THE SKY LOOKS VERY FLUFFY TONIGHT!

HMMM, ACTUALLY IT'S STARTING TO SNOW!

DON'T WORRY, I DON'T THINK IT WILL GET HEAVIER!

Manuscript: Tea Orsi; Layout: Emilio Urbano; Cleanup: Manuela Razzi; Color: Dario Calabria

BUT SOON...

ERM... WHAT WERE YOU SAYING ABOUT THE SNOW, ELSA?

WELL...

MAYBE WE NEED A SHELTER!

SWOOSH

AND...

WOW!

YOU'RE THE BEST, ELSA!

COME ON! LET'S GO INSIDE!

I'M AFRAID WE WON'T GET TO SEE THE LIGHTS VERY CLEARLY TONIGHT...

... MAYBE LATER!

THE NORTHERN LIGHTS ALWAYS FIND THE WAY TO SURPRISE YOU...

"WHEN WE WERE LITTLE, WE WOULD GO ON PICNICS AT NIGHT WITH OUR PARENTS AND PLAY HIDE 'N' SEEK..."

FOUND YOU!

OH NO! MY HIDING WAS PERFECT!

"ONCE WE SUDDENLY LOOKED UP AND... WE COULDN'T BELIEVE OUR EYES!"

OHHHHH!

IT IS SO COLORFUL!

"THEN ELSA MADE AN ICE STAIR SO WE COULD TRY AND CLIMB TO THE LIGHTS!"

WE KEPT TRYING ALL NIGHT, BUT WE NEVER REACHED THEM.

ONCE THE LIGHTS SURPRISED ME TOO!

"ELSA HAD JUST MADE ME AND I WAS EXPLORING THE NORTH MOUNTAIN..."

I LOVE THIS PLACE!

"... BUT I GOT GOING SO FAST THAT I TUMBLED ALL OVER THE PLACE..."

SWOOOOSH

OOOOOOOOOOH!

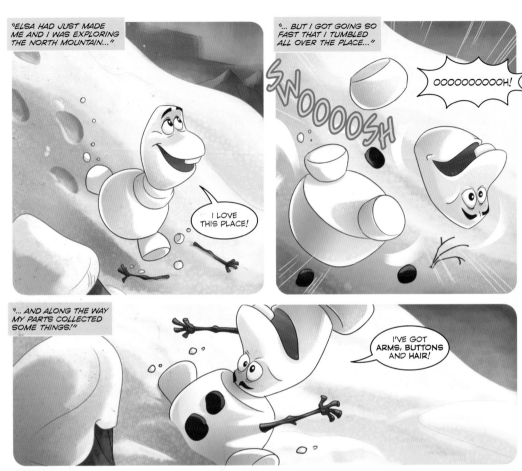

"... AND ALONG THE WAY MY PARTS COLLECTED SOME THINGS!"

I'VE GOT ARMS, BUTTONS AND HAIR!

"AS I GOT MY PARTS INTO THE RIGHT PLACES, THE NORTHERN LIGHTS CAME OUT TO PLAY!"

IT WAS SUCH A **GREAT** SURPRISE!

IT'S GETTING **WINDY**. I'M SURE THE SKY WILL **CLEAR UP** SOON!

WAIT! YOU STILL HAVE TO TELL US YOUR STORY!

DO WE HAVE ONE, SVEN? OH... YES, NOW I REMEMBER!

"ONE NIGHT, SVEN AND I WERE HARVESTING ICE, WHEN WE NOTICED THE LIGHTS REFLECTING ON THE FROZEN GROUND!"

TICK TICK

!

"SVEN IMMEDIATELY TRIED TO CATCH ONE... WITH HIS TONGUE!"

SLAP

OH NO! YOU ARE STUCK!

"I TRIED PUSHING AND PULLING HIM, BUT IT WAS USELESS!"

HMMMMM!

"UNTIL I HAD AN IDEA..."

DON'T WORRY, SVEN! I'M ALMOST DONE!

TICK TICK

"FINALLY SVEN WAS FREE AND THE LIGHTS SEEMED TO CELEBRATE WITH US!"

AMAZING!

WOW! I THINK SOMETHING IS CHANGING OUTSIDE!

LET'S GO AND CHECK!

AND...

SEE? THE LIGHTS SURPRISED US AGAIN!

AND NOW WE HAVE ANOTHER BEAUTIFUL STORY TO REMEMBER FOREVER!

The End

THE TALKING REINDEER

I'D REALLY LIKE TO GIVE ANNA A LITTLE GIFT. WHAT CAN I GET HER, SVEN?

WELL, BUDDY... I—

SHE REALLY LIKES CHOCOLATE!

WHAT?!? YOU CAN SPEAK! IT'S INCREDIBLE.

NO...

IT'S ME! TEE-HEE!

GASP!

SIGH... I THOUGHT IT WAS REALLY SVEN...

WELL, I'M SURE HE WOULD HAVE GIVEN YOU THE SAME SUGGESTION.

Manuscript: Tea Orsi; Layout: Nicoletta Baldari; Color: Dario Calabria

The End

Being a Troll

KRISTOFF AND ANNA HAVE JUST ARRIVED IN TROLL VALLEY, BUT...

HI-YIKES!

HELLOOOOO!

WHOOSH

IT'S SO WINDY TONIGHT!

SPLAT

GASP!

WHOOSH

WE'D BETTER FIND A SHELTER!

HOLD ON!

WE KNOW A GREAT TRICK FOR PROTECTING OURSELVES FROM THE WIND!

HUH?!? BEING A TROLL IS JUST GREAT!

YEAH, ESPECIALLY IN THIS WEATHER!

POP

Manuscript: Tea Orsi; Layout: Emilio Urbano; Cleanup: Marino Gentile; Ink: Roberta Zanotta; Color: Dario Calabria

The End

A Lucky Encounter

ARENDELLE. ELSA AND KRISTOFF HAVE TO GET TO THE NORTH MOUNTAIN AS SOON AS POSSIBLE...

FASTER, KRISTOFF!

WHY DO YOU NEED TO REACH THE NORTH MOUNTAIN?

A COUPLE OF **MOUNTAINEERS** WENT UP THE NORTH MOUNTAIN TWO DAYS AGO AND HAVE NOT COME BACK YET.

I'M WORRIED.

I WANT TO BE SURE THEY ARE SAFE...

"... AND ASK **MARSHMALLOW** *IF HE'S SEEN THEM."*

I THINK THE ANSWER'S YES!

OH NO! MARSHMALLOW'S CHASING THEM!

Manuscript: Alessandro Ferrari; Layout: Nicoletta Baldari; Cleanup: Marino Gentile; Ink: Michela Frare; Color: Stefania Santi

STOP! DON'T!

QUEEN ELSA?

WHAT ARE YOU DOING?

WE WERE CHASING EACH OTHER! IT WAS A GAME! YOU SPOILED THE FUN.

GAME? WHAT GAME?

ARE YOU TRYING TO SAY MARSHMALLOW HASN'T KEPT YOU HERE AGAINST YOUR WILL ALL THIS TIME?

ABSOLUTELY NOT! WE ARE GREAT FRIENDS!

WE SPENT TWO DAYS PLAYING WITH HIM AND HAVING A LOT OF FUN. HE'S THE BEST SNOWMAN WE'VE EVER MET!

WELL... I SUPPOSE I WAS WRONG THIS TIME!

The End

A Snowy Spring

Part 1

IT'S A GLORIOUS MORNING IN THE KINGDOM!

ANNA PLANNED TO SPEND THE DAY WITH HER SISTER, ELSA, AND SOME NEW FRIENDS, BUT...

WHAT IS IT?

I'M NOT SURE.

KAI, WHAT'S GOING ON?

THE VILLAGERS ARE HERE TO SEE YOU, YOUR MAJESTY. THEY'RE SEEKING AN AUDIENCE WITH THE QUEEN. THEY WANT YOUR HELP.

Original Story: Erica David; Manuscript Adaptation: Alessandro Ferrari; Layout: Benedetta Barone; Clean: Benedetta Barone; Color: MichelAngela World

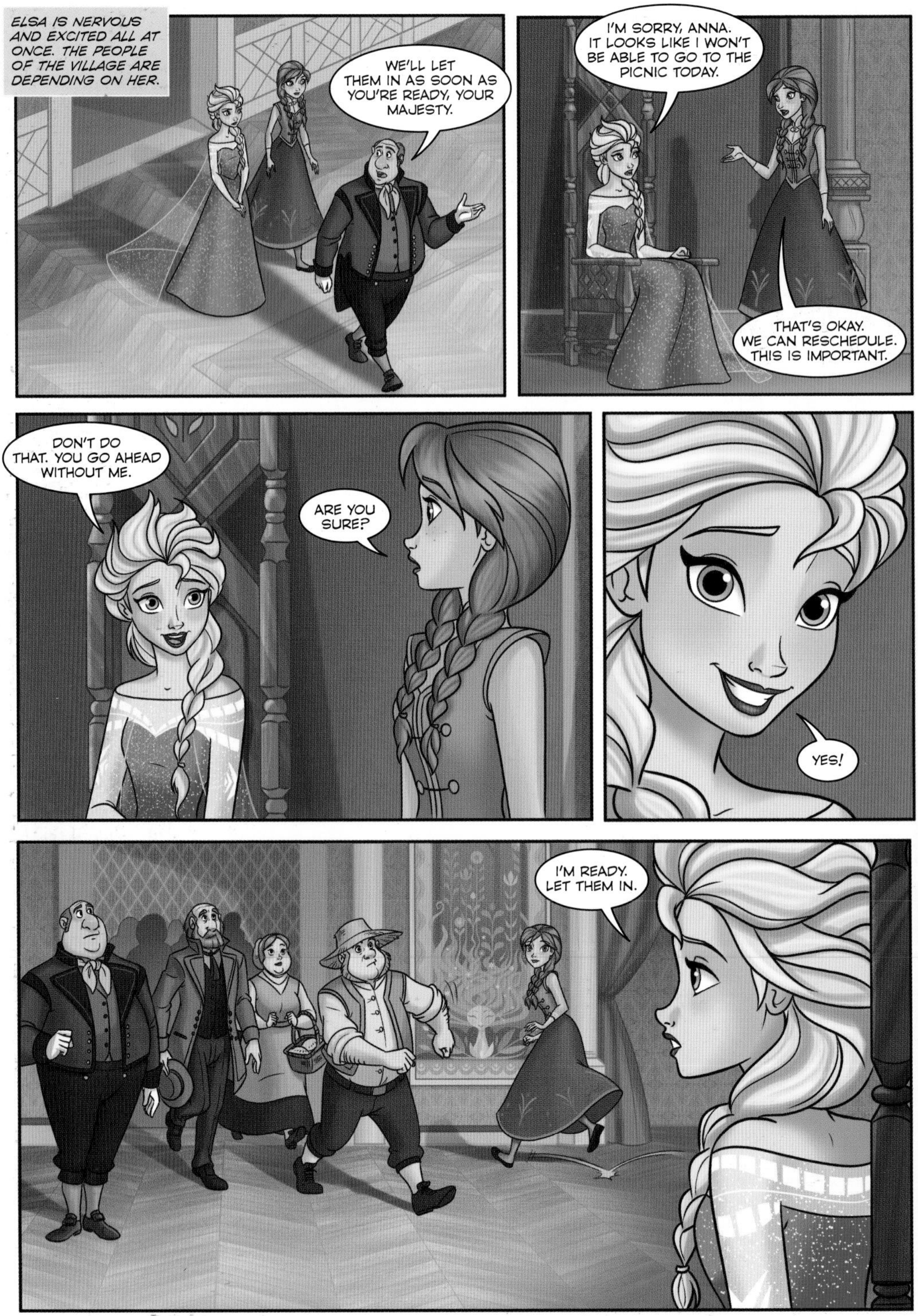
ELSA IS NERVOUS AND EXCITED ALL AT ONCE. THE PEOPLE OF THE VILLAGE ARE DEPENDING ON HER.
WE'LL LET THEM IN AS SOON AS YOU'RE READY, YOUR MAJESTY.
I'M SORRY, ANNA. IT LOOKS LIKE I WON'T BE ABLE TO GO TO THE PICNIC TODAY.
THAT'S OKAY. WE CAN RESCHEDULE. THIS IS IMPORTANT.
DON'T DO THAT. YOU GO AHEAD WITHOUT ME.
ARE YOU SURE?
YES!
I'M READY. LET THEM IN.

GOOD DAY, YOUR MAJESTY. IT'S AN HONOR TO MEET YOU.

IT'S NICE TO MEET YOU, TOO. WHAT BRINGS YOU HERE?

LATELY, WE'VE HAD WONDERFUL WEATHER IN ARENDELLE... FOR PEOPLE. BUT ALL THOSE DAYS OF SUNSHINE HAVE BEEN HARD ON MY BRUSSELS SPROUTS.

HOW CAN I HELP?

MY SPROUTS TASTE MUCH BETTER AFTER A THIN COATING OF SNOW, YOUR MAJESTY.

I THOUGHT YOU MIGHT BE ABLE TO... YOU KNOW.

WHEN YOU RETURN HOME, JUST SPREAD THE SNOW AROUND YOUR FIELDS.

THANK YOU, YOUR MAJESTY!

THE NEXT VILLAGER IN LINE IS A PIE MAKER NAMED TILDA...

IF THEY SIT TOO LONG, MY BANANA CREAMS SPOIL AND MY MERINGUES MELT.

I MAKE A LOT OF PIES, YOUR MAJESTY. BUT I HAVE NOWHERE TO KEEP THEM UNTIL THEY'RE SOLD.

WHAT ABOUT AN ICEBOX?

I WOULD LOVE AN ICEBOX! BUT I CAN'T AFFORD ONE. BESIDES, NONE OF THE ICEBOXES I'VE SEEN ARE LARGE ENOUGH FOR ALL MY PIES.

PUT YOUR PIES IN THIS. THAT SHOULD KEEP THEM FRESH.

OH, THANK YOU, YOUR MAJESTY! NOW I HAVE MY VERY OWN ICEBOX.

ELSA SPENDS THE ENTIRE MORNING HELPING THE PEOPLE OF ARENDELLE. THE VILLAGERS ARE VERY NICE AND VERY GRATEFUL.

BUT SHE HAS TO ADMIT SHE IS GROWING TIRED...

HOO-HOO! MY NAME'S OAKEN.

LOVELY TO SEE YOU AGAIN, OAKEN. HOW CAN I HELP YOU TODAY?

I WANT TO BUILD AN ICE ROOM FOR MY CUSTOMERS. THAT WAY THEY CAN COOL DOWN QUICKLY AFTER THE SAUNA.

AN ENTIRE ROOM MADE OUT OF ICE? ARE YOU SURE?

JA!

ELSA AGREES AND THEY SET TO WORK DRAWING UP PLANS FOR THE ICE ROOM...

HOO-HOO.

...THEN THEY DECIDE THAT SHE WILL GO TO THE TRADING POST TO HELP BUILD IT.

BUT THE LINE OF VILLAGERS IS STILL STRETCHING INTO THE COURTYARD!

IT'S GOING TO BE A LONG AFTERNOON...

MEANWHILE, ANNA IS HAVING A PICNIC WITH HER NEW FRIENDS LISE, THEA, AND SIGRID...

WHERE'S YOUR SISTER? I PACKED LUNCH FOR FIVE.

SHE COULDN'T MAKE IT. SHE HAD SOME... QUEEN STUFF TO DO.

IT CAN'T BE EASY TO BE THE QUEEN. I BET THERE'S A LOT TO DO.

TELL ME ABOUT IT! WHEN I LEFT THIS MORNING, THERE WAS A WHOLE LINE OF PEOPLE WAITING FOR ELSA TO HELP THEM...

WHO HELPS QUEEN ELSA?

!

SUDDENLY...

SNOW?! DOES THAT USUALLY HAPPEN?

NOT AT THIS TIME OF YEAR...

ELSA NEEDS ME!

WHAT WILL HAPPEN NOW? FIND OUT IN THE SECOND PART OF THIS MAGICAL ADVENTURE!

146

End of Part 1

A SNOWY SPRING

Part 2

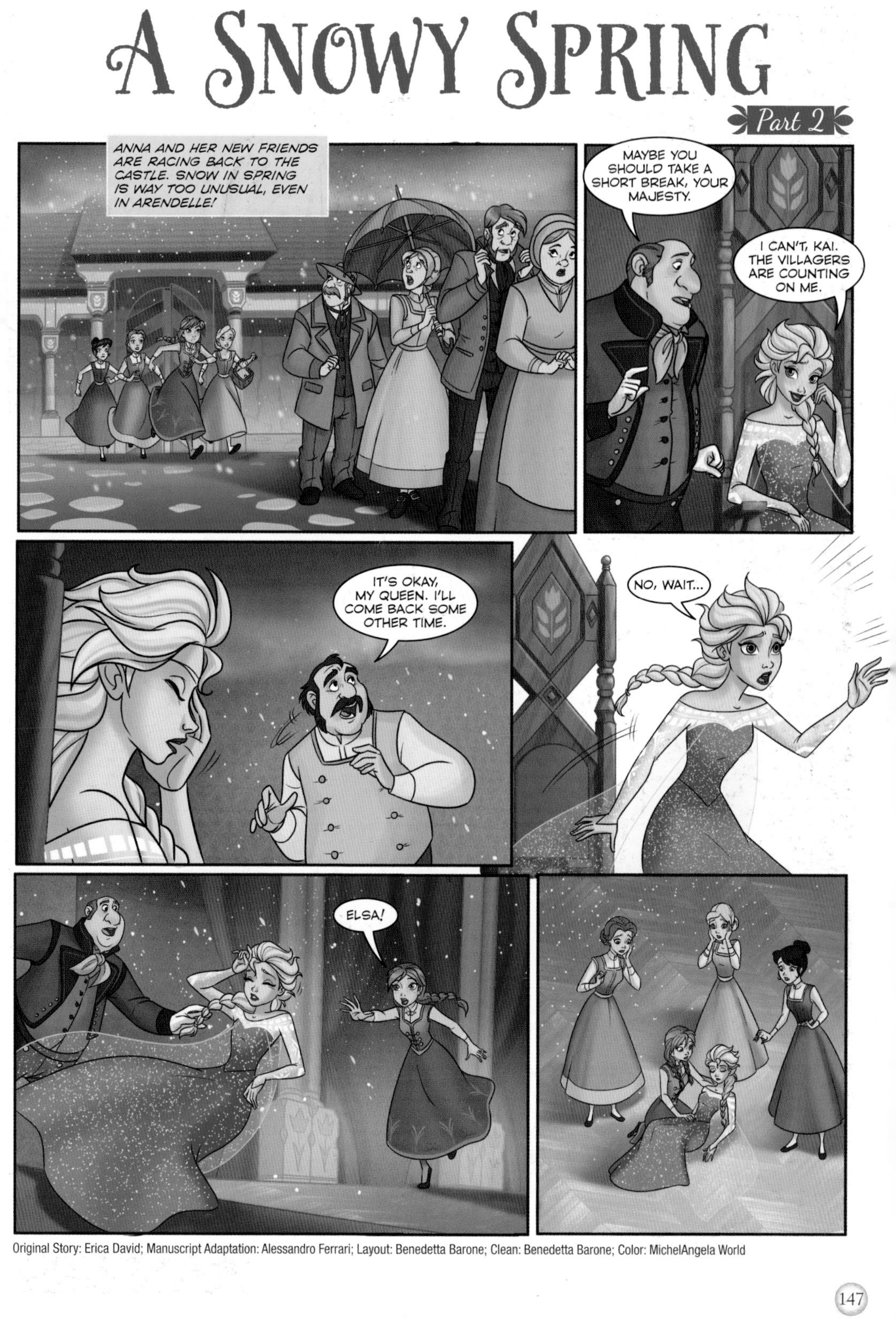
ANNA AND HER NEW FRIENDS ARE RACING BACK TO THE CASTLE. SNOW IN SPRING IS WAY TOO UNUSUAL, EVEN IN ARENDELLE!
MAYBE YOU SHOULD TAKE A SHORT BREAK, YOUR MAJESTY.
I CAN'T, KAI. THE VILLAGERS ARE COUNTING ON ME.
IT'S OKAY, MY QUEEN. I'LL COME BACK SOME OTHER TIME.
NO, WAIT...
ELSA!

Original Story: Erica David; Manuscript Adaptation: Alessandro Ferrari; Layout: Benedetta Barone; Clean: Benedetta Barone; Color: MichelAngela World

I JUST GOT SO TIRED.

I KNOW. THAT'S WHY YOU SHOULD TAKE THE DAY OFF.

I CAN'T. THE PEOPLE OF ARENDELLE ARE DEPENDING ON ME. THEY NEED ME TO USE MY POWERS.

I GET IT. YOUR POWERS ARE VERY COOL— LITERALLY! BUT YOU'RE ALSO STRONG, AND SMART, AND THE WORLD'S BEST BIG SISTER!

THERE ARE PLENTY OF OTHER WAYS FOR YOU TO HELP THE VILLAGERS!

YOU'RE ABSOLUTELY RIGHT, ANNA.

SO...

WHAT IF I HAVE MY ROYAL CARPENTERS BUILD YOU A LARGE ICEBOX OUT OF WOOD OR STONE? YOU CAN BUY ICE BLOCKS FROM THE HARVESTERS AND PUT THEM INSIDE THE BOX TO KEEP YOUR FISH COLD.

BUT...

I WAS HOPING YOU WOULD MAKE ME A BOX WITH YOUR MAGIC...

HELPING THE VILLAGERS WITHOUT USING HER POWERS IS HARDER THAN SHE THOUGHT IT WOULD BE...

OF COURSE I CAN MAKE YOU A BOX. IT'S NO TROUBLE AT ALL.

BUT MAGIC IS JUST ONE PART OF ELSA, AND IF MAGIC IS ALL THE PEOPLE EXPECT, THEY WILL NEVER TRULY KNOW HER.'

MY NAME IS DAGMAR, AND I RUN THE VILLAGE LAUNDRY, YOUR MAJESTY.

LATELY, THERE HAVE BEEN MORE AND MORE DIRTY CLOTHES, AND I CAN'T GET ENOUGH WATER TO CLEAN THEM. IS THERE ANY WAY YOUR MAGIC COULD HELP WITH THE WATER?

REMEMBER... THERE ARE OTHER WAYS TO HELP THE PEOPLE OF ARENDELLE.

I HAVE PLANS FOR ARENDELLE'S NEW PLUMBING SYSTEM. THE PIPES AND CANALS WILL CARRY WATER ALL ACROSS THE VILLAGE. YOU'LL BE ABLE TO DRAW WATER RIGHT AT THE LAUNDRY!

DO YOU THINK YOU CAN DO THIS?

WE CAN DO THIS. THIS PLUMBING SYSTEM WILL BENEFIT EVERYONE. IF EVERYONE PITCHES IN, WE CAN BUILD THE WATER PUMP IN A DAY!

WHO WILL HELP ME?

I'LL HELP!

ME TOO!

I'LL HELP!

COUNT ME IN!

THE NEXT DAY, THE WORK BEGINS. AND EVERYONE HELPS...

FRESH-SQUEEZED LEMONADE!

YOU WERE RIGHT, ANNA. I LOVE USING MY MAGIC TO HELP PEOPLE. BUT SOME DAYS, HELPING THEM THIS WAY IS EVEN BETTER.

WAY TO WIN THEIR HEARTS!

I DON'T KNOW HOW TO THANK YOU!

I DO!

THREE CHEERS FOR QUEEN ELSA!

ALL HAIL THE QUEEN!

ALL HAIL THE QUEEN!

ALL HAIL THE QUEEN!

151

I HOPE YOU DON'T MIND, BUT I GAVE THE VILLAGERS THE DAY OFF.

THE VILLAGERS DON'T NEED A DAY OFF.

BUT YOU DO.

ANNA, WE'VE BEEN OVER THIS. YOU KNOW I HAVE RESPONSIBILITIES. THE PEOPLE OF ARENDELLE ARE DEPENDING ON ME.

I KNOW. THAT'S WHY KAI AND I HAVE WORKED OUT A SCHEDULE. THE PEOPLE OF ARENDELLE WILL VISIT THE PALACE THREE DAYS A WEEK...

THE OTHER DAYS ARE FOR YOUR OTHER DUTIES, LIKE SPENDING TIME WITH YOUR SISTER!

The End

ICY TRICK

Manuscript: Tea Orsi; Layout and cleanup: Nicoletta Baldari; Color: Dario Calabria

ELSA CREATES AN ICE LAYER ON THE FLOOR.

LET ME TRY!

SWOOOSH

YAY!

IT'S TIME FOR SOME TIDYING UP FUN!

SWISH

I LOVE SLIDING ON ICE!

AND THIS WAY IT'S EASIER TO TIDY UP!

CLACK

AND IT'S QUICK! WE USED TO DO IT ALL THE TIME WHEN WE WERE LITTLE!

NOW WE CAN DO THIS EVERY TIME MY ROOM IS MESSY!

YOU MEAN EVERY DAY, DON'T YOU?

The End

GONE FISHING!

BEHOLD! *A FISHING HOLE.* THE FINEST YOU'LL EVER FIND ON THE FJORD!

OOH! OOH! I CAN'T *WAIT* TO TRY IT!

WHOA, WHOA, OLAF! FISHING IS ABOUT *MORE* THAN JUST DROPPING A LINE IN THE WATER...

...THERE'S A *SCIENCE* TO THIS THAT'S BEEN PASSED DOWN THROUGH GENERATIONS OF FISHERMEN. FIRST THINGS FIRST--

--WE HAVE TO PET JØRGEN.

HOW *SAD.* HE FORGOT YOUR *NAME.*

NO, I MEAN JØRGEN...

...THE *GOOD LUCK CHARM* BULDA MADE FOR ME WHEN I WAS A KID. IT'S ALWAYS HELPED ME CATCH FISH. I NEVER LEAVE HOME WITHOUT IT--

NYAAA!

CHOMP!

Manuscript: Joe Caramagna; Layout: Ciro Cangialosi; Pencil: Letizia Algeri; Paint: Stefania Santi

155

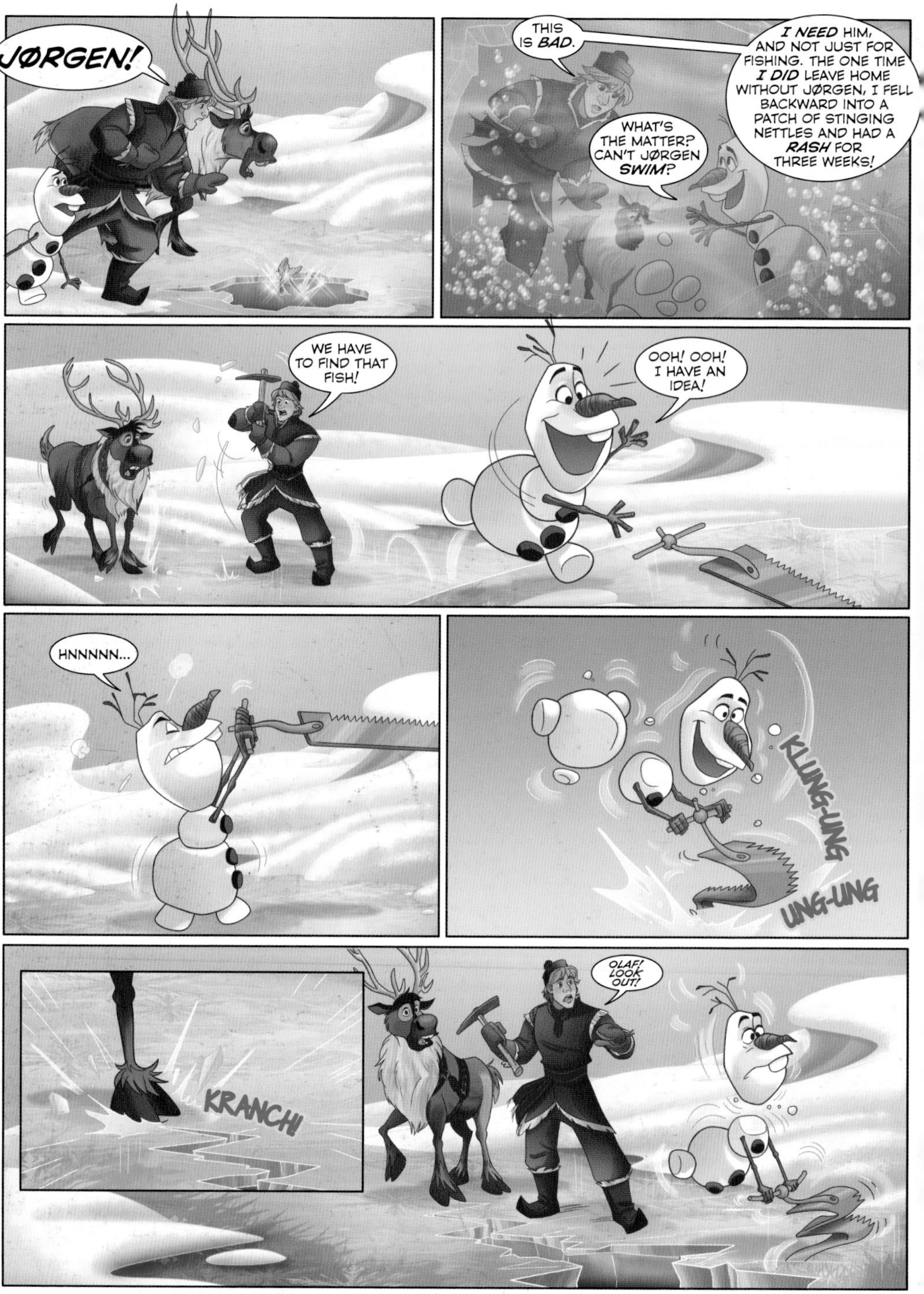
JØRGEN!
THIS IS BAD.
I NEED HIM, AND NOT JUST FOR FISHING. THE ONE TIME I DID LEAVE HOME WITHOUT JØRGEN, I FELL BACKWARD INTO A PATCH OF STINGING NETTLES AND HAD A RASH FOR THREE WEEKS!
WHAT'S THE MATTER? CAN'T JØRGEN SWIM?
WE HAVE TO FIND THAT FISH!
OOH! OOH! I HAVE AN IDEA!
HNNNNN...
KLUNG-UNG
UNG-UNG
KRANCH!
OLAF! LOOK OUT!

HELP!

SPLASSH!

OLAF!

BLRRRRRRRGH!

BLEY *NNN BLOO!*

GOT YOU!

AND *YOU*, TOO!

I CAUGHT MY FIRST FISH!

SPAK!

PLISH!

ARE YOU GOING TO USE YOUR LUCKY CHARM AGAIN?

NOT TODAY...I THINK I HAVE ANOTHER IDEA. THE FISH *REALLY* SEEMED TO LIKE... YOUR *NOSE*.

NOT *YOUR* NOSE, BUT...

MY *NOSE?!* BUT I KINDA LIKE MY NOSE....

...CARROTS!

The End

MYSTERIOUS RECORD

Manuscript: Tea Orsi; Layout: Alberto Zanon; Cleanup: Marino Gentile; Ink: Michela Frare; Color: Stefania Santi

The End

Always Prepared

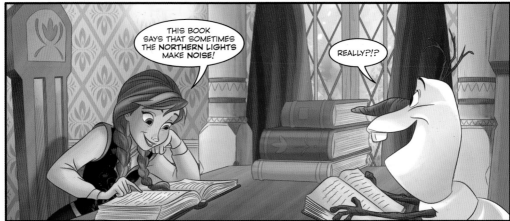

THIS BOOK SAYS THAT SOMETIMES THE NORTHERN LIGHTS MAKE NOISE!

REALLY?!?

I'VE NEVER HEARD THEM!

ME NEITHER! I WONDER WHAT THEY SOUND LIKE!

SO WE NEED VERY BIG EARS?

KIND OF... I THINK OAKEN CAN HELP US!

THAT NIGHT, AFTER VISITING OAKEN...

HUH?!? I THOUGHT YOU WERE LOOKING AT THE LIGHTS...

NO, TONIGHT WE ARE LISTENING TO THEM!

Manuscript: Tea Orsi; Layout: Manuela Razzi; Cleanup: Marino Gentile; Ink: Michela Frare; Color: Stefania Santi

The End

A Trip Through the Sky

CAN'T YOU TELL ME WHAT THIS IS ALL ABOUT?

YOU'LL SEE IN JUST A MOMENT...

"WE'VE BEEN WORKING ON THIS FOR WEEKS..."

"...KEEPING IT A SECRET FROM EVERYONE."

"ESPECIALLY FROM YOU, SINCE WE WANTED IT TO BE A SURPRISE."

Manuscript: Alessandro Ferrari; Layout: Alberto Zanon; Cleanup: Benedetta Barone; Color: MichelAngela World

AND HERE IT IS... OUR FIRST HOT-AIR BALLOON! ISN'T IT GREAT?!

YES, IT IS!

DESIGNED AND BUILT BY ANNA!

COME ON, LET'S GIVE IT A TRY!

RIGHT NOW?

YOU BET! LET'S GET IN. OAKEN SAYS IT WILL BE COLD UP THERE. I KNOW IT DOESN'T BOTHER YOU, BUT I'M BRINGING THESE BLANKETS.

HOO-HOO. ENJOY YOUR FLIGHT!

BYE, OAKEN! BYE, SVEN! YOU'RE GETTING SMALLER... AND SMALLER.

WOW, WHAT A BEAUTIFUL VIEW OF ARENDELLE!

I CAN STILL SEE MY FRIENDS! HELLO, FRIENDS!

FLYING LIKE THIS IS AMAZING, ANNA!

EVEN THOUGH IT'S A BIT WINDIER THAN WE EXPECTED...

SPEAKING OF WHICH... LOOK!

THIS WIND IS BLOWING US TOWARD THAT MOUNTAIN!

WE'VE GOT TO LAND SOON OR WE'LL CRASH INTO IT!

THAT SNOW-COVERED HILL LOOKS LIKE A SOFT LANDING SPOT!

TURN OFF THE FIRE!

DONE! HANG ON!

WE'RE TOO CLOSE. WE'RE NOT GOING DOWN FAST ENOUGH!

IT LOOKS FAR TO ME!

WE NEED TO WEIGH THE BALLOON DOWN!

EXACTLY! AND I KNOW HOW!

KRISTOFF, TIE THE BLANKETS ON THE OTHER SIDE! ELSA, GET READY TO FILL THEM!

FILL THEM?!

CAN YOU MAKE SOME ICE?

IT'S WORKING. WE'RE GOING DOWN!

IT FEELS MORE LIKE FALLING...

...FALLING FAST!

HOLD ON!

THUMPH

IS EVERYONE OKAY?

OH, YEAH! AND...

...THAT WAS INCREDIBLE!

LET'S DO IT AGAIN!

I'M IN! BUT NEXT TIME I'M BRINGING SVEN, TOO!

AND NEXT TIME I'LL BE PREPARED! HAHAHA!

The End

A Snowflakes Surprise

Manuscript: Tea Orsi; Layout: Elisabetta Melaranci;
Cleanup: Nicoletta Baldari; Color: Dario Calabria

The End

A Great Strategy

IT'S A GREAT DAY TO PLAY ICE HOCKEY...

CAN I PLAY TOO?

OF COURSE, OLAF!

JUST WATCH OUT FOR BODY CHECKS!

YES, WE CAN BLOCK YOU TO PREVENT YOU FROM SCORING!

LIKE THIS! BUT YOU KEEP GOING AND PROTECT THE PUCK!

OKAY, I'M READY!

SWISH

WOAH... WHAT ARE YOU--

W-WAIT!

AM I DOING IT RIGHT?

TUMP

ALMOST, OLAF!

I THINK YOU'VE FOUND A NEW STRATEGY!

Manuscript: Tea Orsi; Layout: Alberto Zanon; Cleanup: Marino Gentile; Ink: Michela Frare; Color: Stefania Santi

The End

The Mysterious Trickster

A VILLAGER NEEDS ANNA AND ELSA'S HELP...

LAST NIGHT SOMEONE VISITED MY GARDEN AND... ALMOST DESTROYED IT!

WHAT A MESS!

WHO WOULD DO SOMETHING SO TERRIBLE?

IT MUST BE THE SAME ONE WHO TOOK MY LAUNDRY!

REALLY?!?

TELL US MORE!

LAST NIGHT I LEFT THE LAUNDRY OUTSIDE AND SOMEONE SCATTERED IT ALL OVER THE GARDEN!

OH, NO!

DON'T WORRY! WE'LL INVESTIGATE.

OH, THANK YOU!

Manuscript: Tea Orsi; Layout: Emilio Urbano; Cleanup: Manuela Razzi and MichelAngela World; Ink and Color: MichelAngela World

SO... WHERE SHOULD WE START?

WE NEED TO WAIT AND SEE IF THE TRICKSTER STRIKES AGAIN... MAYBE TONIGHT!

ANNA! ELSA! HEEEEY!

I THINK WE COULD USE SOME HELP!

ARE YOU READY TO HELP US WITH AN INVESTIGATION?

YEEEES!

WHAT'S AN INVESTIGATION?

THE GROUP FIGURES OUT A PLAN, AND AT SUNSET...

OKAY, EACH OF US WILL COVER A DIFFERENT AREA!

WATCH OUT FOR ANY SUSPICIOUS MOVEMENT!

SOON IT GETS DARK AND...

GASP! THAT SHADOW LOOKS REALLY FAMILIAR...

I DIDN'T KNOW THE DUKE OF WESELTON WAS BACK IN ARENDELLE!

ERM...

AT THE SAME TIME, KRISTOFF HEARS A STRANGE NOISE BUT...

HUH?!? IT WAS ONLY THE WIND!

SHRRRRIIIEEEEK

WHILE ANNA...

THAT MAN SEEMS TO BE HIDING SOMETHING!

BUT...

OOPS! FALSE ALARM!

ANJA WILL LOVE HER ANNIVERSARY PRESENT!

MEANWHILE, NEAR ANOTHER HOUSE...

IT'S A BABY SVEN!

!

HMMM...I THINK HE LOVES TO PLAY IN GARDENS!

!

LET'S TAKE A BREAK FROM THE INVESTIGATION AND JOIN HIM!

OLAF! DID YOU FIND SOMETHING?

OH, YOU'RE HERE!

WE'VE JUST MET SOMEONE REALLY CUTE!

GOOD JOB! I THINK YOU FOUND OUR TRICKSTER!

YIKES! WHAT A DISASTER!

REALLY?!? WHERE IS IT?

IT'S YOUR LITTLE REINDEER FRIEND, OLAF!

HE PROBABLY GOT LOST AND ENDED UP IN THE VILLAGE.

OOOOH! DO YOU THINK WE CAN KEEP HIM?

PROBABLY NOT, OLAF. I THINK WE NEED TO TAKE HIM BACK TO HIS HERD!

YES, HE NEEDS A BIG MEADOW WHERE HE CAN PLAY...

... FAR FROM LAUNDRY AND YUMMY VEGETABLE GARDENS!

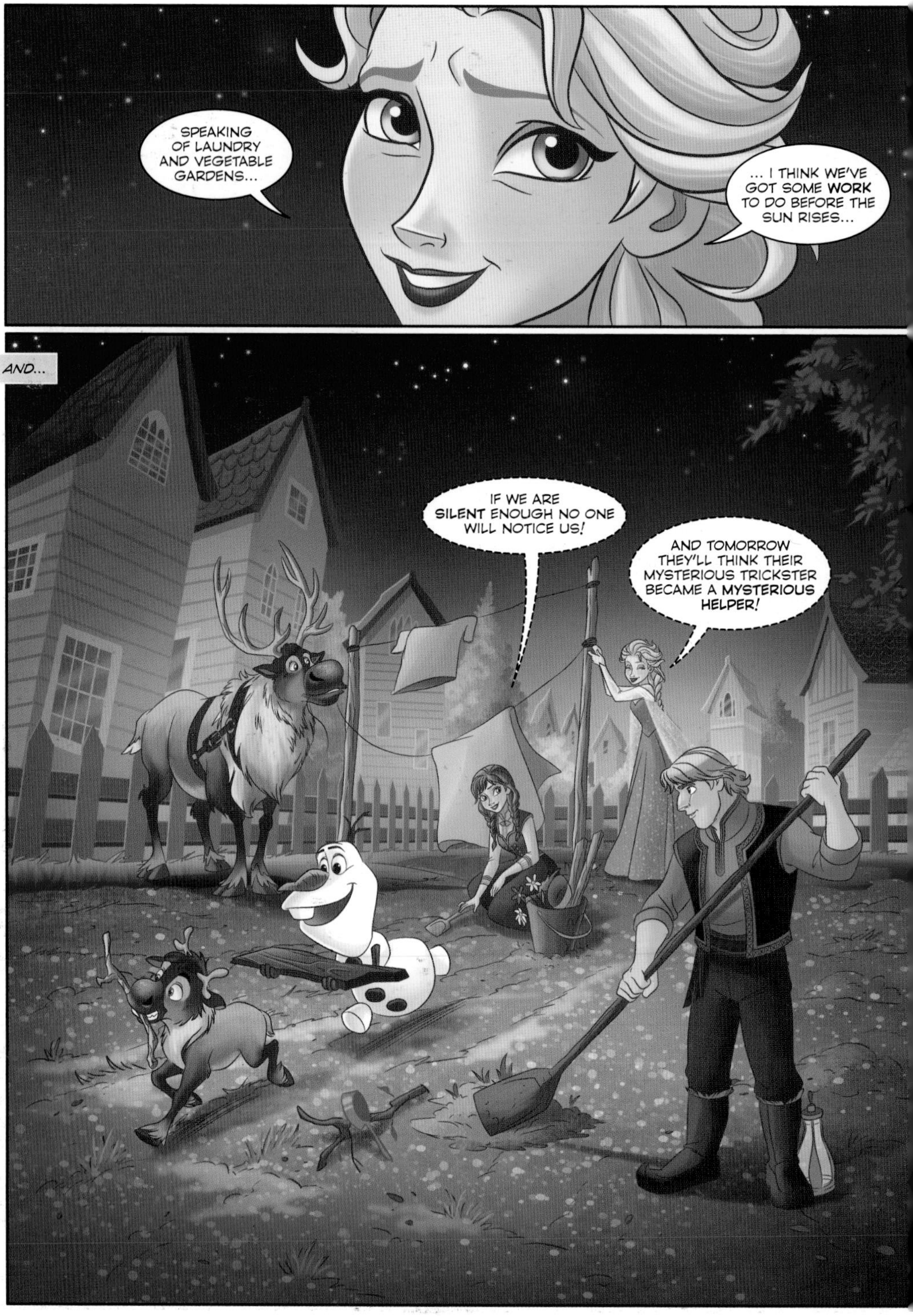
SPEAKING OF LAUNDRY AND VEGETABLE GARDENS...
... I THINK WE'VE GOT SOME **WORK** TO DO BEFORE THE SUN RISES...
AND...
IF WE ARE **SILENT** ENOUGH NO ONE WILL NOTICE US!
AND TOMORROW THEY'LL THINK THEIR MYSTERIOUS TRICKSTER BECAME A **MYSTERIOUS HELPER**!

The End

THE BEST COMPROMISE

ITTLE KRISTOFF AND BABY SVEN USED TO LIVE WITH THE TROLLS...

BULDA, WHY ARE WE SO DIFFERENT FROM YOU TROLLS?

BEING DIFFERENT IS JUST GREAT, KRISTOFF!

YOU ARE A SPECIAL KIND OF TROLL WHO CAN PLAY JUST LIKE US!

AND YOU CAN ALSO WEAR OUR MOSS CLOAKS!

I KNOW, BUT...

WE CAN'T TURN INTO ROCKS!

OH, DEAR! BUT YOU'RE LUCKY TO BE AWAKE DURING THE DAY!

LET'S TRY TO TURN INTO ROCKS!

?!?

Manuscript: Tea Orsi; Layout: Emilio Urbano; Cleanup: Caterina Giorgetti; Color: MichelAngela World

SO, WHEN THE SUN RISES...

IT'S TIME!

LET'S ROLL UP LIKE REAL TROLLS!

?

BUT SOON...

REMEMBER WE CAN'T MOVE! WE ARE ROCKS NOW!

A HARE! I'D REALLY LIKE TO PLAY WITH IT, BUT...ROCKS DON'T RUN!

BOING BOING

!

YOU KNOW WHAT? BULDA WAS RIGHT! WE ARE SPECIAL TROLLS!

WE ARE LUCKY BECAUSE WE GET TO HAVE FUN DURING THE DAY!

!

The End

THE ARENDELLE CUP

EVERY YEAR PEOPLE FROM ALL OVER THE WORLD TAKE PART IN THE ARENDELLE CUP, A SLED RACE THAT LASTS THREE DAYS.

WELCOME TO ARENDELLE!

THE TEAM FROM **ELDORA**, THE DESERT KINGDOM, IS MADE UP OF **NINA** AND **NAIA**...

ARENDELLE'S CLIMATE IS SO DIFFERENT FROM ELDORA'S.

YOU HAVE ALL KINDS OF PLANTS WE'VE NEVER SEEN!

AND YOU MUST BE TASHI AND TENZIN FROM CHATHO!

WE ARE! IT'S A PLEASURE TO MEET YOU.

WE'VE BROUGHT A PRESENT FROM QUEEN COLISA.

WHEN WE'RE NOT **RACING YAKS**, WE LOVE TO SCULPT.

A CHATHAN SLOTH! WHAT A BEAUTIFUL GIFT!

Original story by Erica David; Adapted by Tea Orsi; Layout: Manuela Razzi and Marino Gentile; Clean: Marino Gentile; Color: MichelAngela World

YOUR MAJESTY, I AM LEOPOLD OF WESELTON. MAY I HAVE THIS DANCE?

LUTZ AND I ARE THE BEST TEAM IN THE WORLD. YOU CAN'T WIN!

TIME WILL TELL. WE MIGHT NOT HAVE RACED BEFORE, BUT WE'VE PRACTICED HARD.

MAYBE, BUT YOU'LL NEED SOME GOOD LUCK, TOO!

OH... THANK YOU.

WE'LL PROVE THEM WRONG.

YES! WE HAVE A LOT OF EXPERIENCE WITH ICE AND SNOW. HEHEHE!

SIVOY AND SUQI FROM TIKAANI! YOU'RE THE DEFENDING CHAMPIONS!

THEY SAY YOU KNOW EVERYTHING ABOUT RACING!

I WOULDN'T SAY "EVERYTHING." EACH RACE IS DIFFERENT.

THERE'S ALWAYS SOMETHING NEW TO LEARN.

THE NEXT DAY DAWNS CLEAR AND BRIGHT, AND THE TEAMS PREPARE TO RACE...

AS YOU ALL KNOW, TODAY YOU'LL TRAVEL ACROSS FLAT LAND...

... AND ON DAY TWO YOU'LL HEAD INTO THE MOUNTAINS!

ON YOUR MARKS, GET SET...

WHOOOSH

GO!

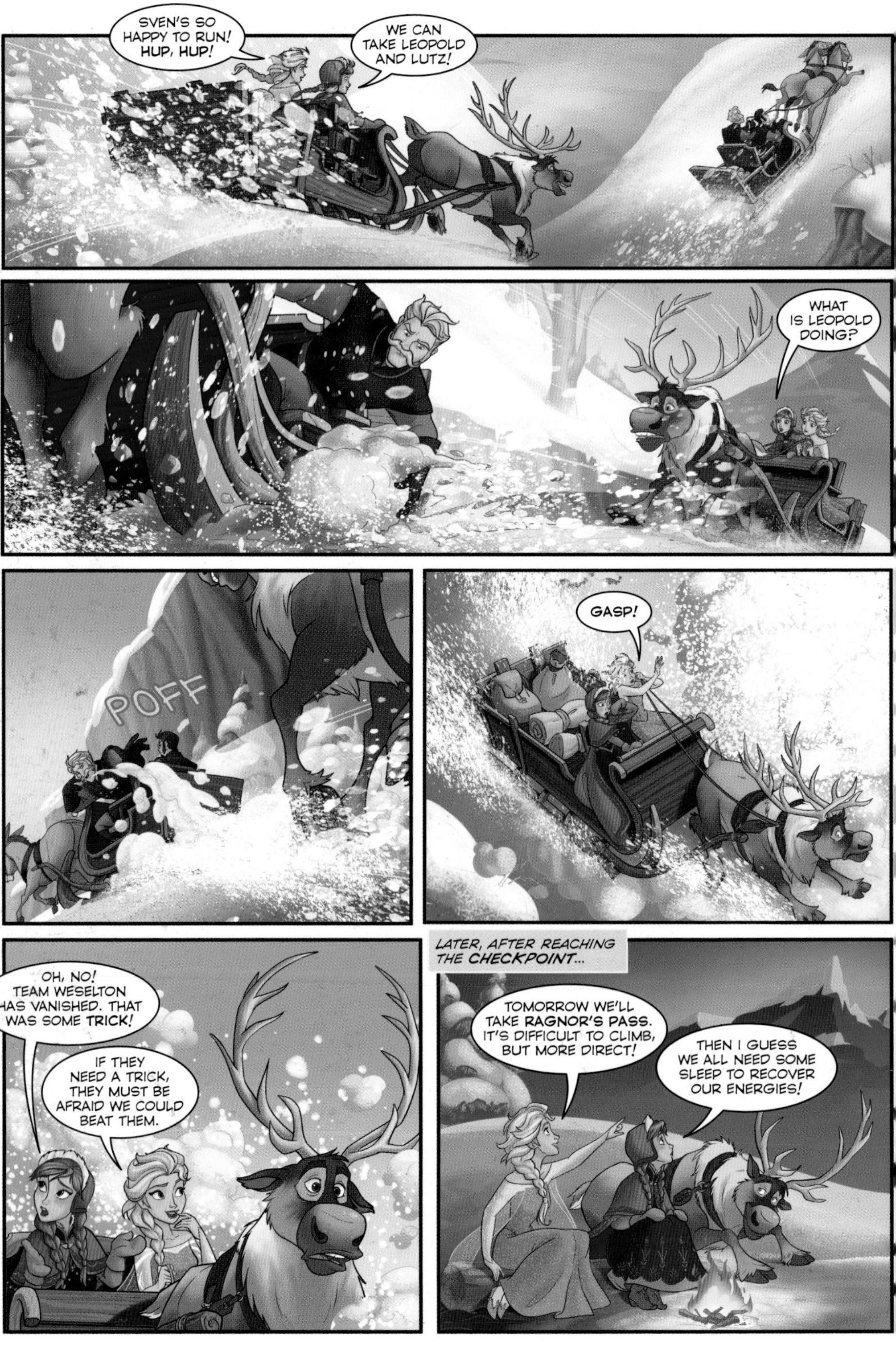
SVEN'S SO HAPPY TO RUN! HUP, HUP!
WE CAN TAKE LEOPOLD AND LUTZ!
WHAT IS LEOPOLD DOING?
POFF
GASP!
OH, NO! TEAM WESELTON HAS VANISHED. THAT WAS SOME TRICK!
IF THEY NEED A TRICK, THEY MUST BE AFRAID WE COULD BEAT THEM.
LATER, AFTER REACHING THE CHECKPOINT...
TOMORROW WE'LL TAKE RAGNOR'S PASS. IT'S DIFFICULT TO CLIMB, BUT MORE DIRECT!
THEN I GUESS WE ALL NEED SOME SLEEP TO RECOVER OUR ENERGIES!

NEXT MORNING, TEAM ARENDELLE SETS OFF VERY EARLY, AND SOON...

DO YOU THINK THE OTHER TEAMS CHOSE THIS STEEP ROUTE, TOO?

I GUESS IT DEPENDS ON HOW WELL THEIR SLEDS CAN HANDLE THE SLOPE.

OF COURSE YOU CAN HANDLE IT, SVEN. BUT WE'LL HELP YOU!

LATER...

NINA? NAIA? WHAT HAPPENED?

OUR HORSE BROWNIE IS SICK.

HE ATE THIS PLANT ALONG THE TRAIL AND HAS A STOMACHACHE.

HELVIG'S HOLLY! SNEEZEWORT TEA WILL MAKE HIM FEEL BETTER. I KNOW HOW TO MAKE IT, BUT I DON'T THINK WE PACKED ANY.

WE PICKED A CLUSTER OF SNEEZEWORT YESTERDAY! BUT WE DON'T WANT TO SLOW YOU DOWN IN THE RACE...

SOME THINGS ARE MORE IMPORTANT THAN RACING.

AFTER NURSING BROWNIE, THE TWO TEAMS REACH THE CHECKPOINT TIED FOR LAST PLACE.

SVEN IS ACTING STRANGE TONIGHT.

HE'S DEFINITELY TRYING TO **TELL** US SOMETHING...

SNORT!

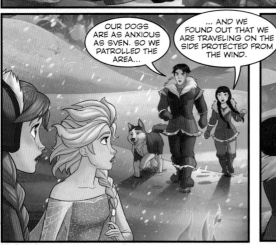

OUR DOGS ARE AS ANXIOUS AS SVEN. SO WE PATROLLED THE AREA...

... AND WE FOUND OUT THAT WE ARE TRAVELING ON THE SIDE PROTECTED FROM THE WIND.

BUT THE MOST IMPORTANT FACT IS THAT THE **SNOWFLAKES** ARE NEEDLE-SHAPED. LOOK!

OH THEY'RE BEAUTIFUL!

BUT DANGEROUS! THIS SHAPE AND THE SNOW PLUMES I SAW, ARE SIGNS OF AN AVALANCHE.

WHAT WILL HAPPEN? WILL THE TEAMS AVOID THE DANGER? YOU'LL FIND OUT SOON.

SO THAT'S WHAT SVEN WAS TRYING TO TELL US!

WE SHOULD WARN THE OTHERS!

End of Part 1

THE ARENDELLE CUP

Part 2

TEAM TIKAANI WARNS ALL THE TEAMS ABOUT THE DANGER. BUT THE NEXT MORNING...

IS SOMETHING WRONG?

EVERYONE'S HERE **EXCEPT** THE TEAM FROM **WESELTON**.

WE SHOULD TAKE INGRID'S LEAP, BUT WE SAW **HOOFPRINTS** LEADING TO THE PASS...

SO LUTZ AND LEOPOLD LEFT BEFORE US!

THEY'LL GET CAUGHT IN THE **AVALANCHE!**

WE HAVE TO GO AFTER THEM!

MAYBE THEY WOULDN'T DO THE SAME FOR US. BUT WE **CAN'T** LET THEM GET HURT...

ELSA'S RIGHT. WE'LL LOOK OUT FOR EACH OTHER AND MAKE SURE TEAM WESELTON IS SAFE.

LET'S FOLLOW THE MULE TRACKS!

Original story by Erica David; Adapted by Tea Orsi; Layout: Manuela Razzi and Marino Gentile; Clean: Marino Gentile; Color: MichelAngela World

I THINK THOSE SLOPES ARE ABOUT TO GIVE WAY.

CAREFUL! WE NEED TO SLOW DOWN!

ANY SUDDEN MOVEMENT CAN CAUSE THE SNOW TO SLIDE.

BUT...

ROOOOARRRRR

OH NO!

I KNOW WHAT I HAVE TO DO...

SWOOOSH

DON'T WORRY!
I'LL RAISE SOME
MORE WALLS!

I DON'T THINK
IT'S GOING TO
HOLD, ELSA!

SWOOSH

WITHIN SECONDS,
ELSA BUILDS AN
ICE SHELTER...

YOU SAVED US!

WE DIDN'T KNOW
YOUR POWERS WERE
SO AMAZING!

A FEW MINUTES LATER...

THE AVALANCHE IS OVER! LET'S KEEP LOOKING FOR TEAM WESELTON.

I HOPE THEY'RE SAFE...

THE MULE TRACKS—THEY'RE GONE!

WHAT ARE WE GOING TO DO?

KAYA HAS BEEN TRAINED TO FIND PEOPLE LOST IN THE SNOW.

LEOPOLD GAVE ME THIS GOLDEN ACORN! IT CAN HELP HER TRACE HIS SCENT!

PERFECT! I'M SURE SHE WILL FIND THEM!

SNIFF SNIFF

KAYA STARTS SNIFFING THE GROUND AND THE TEAMS FOLLOW HER, UNTIL...

CREA!

DO YOU HEAR THAT?

IT SOUNDS ALMOST LIKE WOOD CREAKING BENEATH US.

MAYBE IT'S TEAM WESELTON! LET ME SEE!

SWISH

CREAK

LOOK!

IT MUST BE THEM! OR AT LEAST THEIR SLED.

THEY MIGHT BE TRAPPED UNDERNEATH!

HOW CAN WE GET THEM OUT?

WE CAN HELP! AS YOU KNOW, WE ARE SCULPTORS.

BRILLIANT! YOU CAN CHISEL THE ICE AWAY.

WE SHOULDN'T HAMMER TOO HARD.

CHOP CHOP

YES, ANY SUDDEN MOVEMENT MAY CAUSE ANOTHER AVALANCHE.

SOON...

YOU FOUND US! WE WERE ON THE PASS WHEN THE AVALANCHE HIT...

WE TOOK COVER UNDER THE SLED, BUT WE WERE RUNNING OUT OF AIR!

YOUR ACORN TRULY BROUGHT US LUCK! WITHOUT IT, KAYA WOULDN'T HAVE TRACED YOU SO QUICKLY.

WE OWE YOU AN APOLOGY. WE WERE SO BUSY CHEATING AND TRYING TO WIN...

AND...

FOR THE FIRST TIME IN THE HISTORY OF THE CUP, ALL FIVE TEAMS HAVE WON! BUT THERE'S AN EVEN BETTER PRIZE THAN THE CUP THIS TIME: NEW FRIENDS!

THE RIGHT SEASON

Manuscript: Tea Orsi; Layout: Emilio Urbano; Cleanup: Nicoletta Baldari; Colore: Dario Calabria

The End

CHATHO'S WONDERS

ANNA AND ELSA HAVE JUST RETURNED FROM A TRIP TO THE LAND OF CHATHO.

SO GOOD TO SEE YOU AGAIN!

WELCOME BACK!

WE MISSED YOU!

DO YOU HAVE MORE BAGS I CAN HELP WITH?

THANKS, KRISTOFF! HOW KIND OF YOU!

WE BROUGHT SOME SOUVENIRS! THEY'RE IN THE CARGO HOLD.

!

I KNOW, I COULDN'T BELIEVE IT EITHER! CHATHO IS A LAND FULL OF WONDERS!

AND YOU BROUGHT THEM ALL HOME WITH YOU!

Manuscript: Valentina Cambi; Layout: Alberto Zanon; Cleanup: Marino Gentile; Ink: Michela Frare; Color: MichelAngela World

The End

A Very Hot Day

IT'S A VERY HOT SUMMER DAY IN ARENDELLE, AND SVEN COULD USE A BIT OF SHADE...

SIGH!

HELLO, SVEN!

ARE YOU ENJOYING THE SUN, TOO?

!

MMM, I LOVE SUMMERTIME!

Manuscript: Tea Orsi; Layout: Manuela Razzi; Cleanup: Veronica Di lorenzo; Paint: Dario Calabria

WHAT'S THE MATTER?

UMPF!

HEY, I LIKE BEING CLOSE TO YOU, TOO!

HUH?! YOU LOOK SO HOT, BUDDY. YOU NEED A SNOW FLURRY TOO.

SIGH!

AND SOON...

NOW THIS SUMMER DAY IS EVEN MORE BEAUTIFUL, ISN'T IT, SVEN?

The End

ONLY AT NIGHT

ONE DAY, AT SUNSET...

SOMETIMES I WONDER HOW THE TROLLS CAN SLEEP ALL DAY LONG...

YOU CAN'T DO MUCH ELSE WHEN YOU ARE A ROCK!

AND...DO THEY DREAM WHEN THEY SLEEP?

WELL, I DON'T KNOW IF THEY DREAM...

BUT SOMEHOW THEY ALWAYS PREPARE FOR A GREAT NIGHT!

THEY DEFINITELY DO!

WELCOME BACK!

LET'S DANCE!

Manuscript: Tea Orsi; Layout: Alberto Zanon; Cleanup: Nicoletta Baldari; Color: Stefania Santi

The End

HIDE 'N' SEEK

ANNA, OLAF AND SVEN HAVE BEEN PLAYING IN THE SNOW ALL DAY. NOW IT'S HIDE 'N' SEEK TIME!

...FORTY-EIGHT, FORTY-NINE...FIFTY! READY OR NOT... HERE I COME!

UH-OH! THERE'S MY BIG FRIEND SVEN!

NOW LET'S SEE WHERE OLAF IS... HUH?!?

HELLO!

HA, HA! THERE YOU ARE!

THE MOST ADORABLE SNOWMAN EVER!

HOW DID YOU FIND ME? I HID SO WELL!

Manuscript: Tea Orsi; Layout: Emilio Urbano; Cleanup: Manuela Razzi; Color: Stefania Santi

The End

JOURNEY TO CHATHO

ANNA AND ELSA ARE LOOKING AT SOME OLD MEMORIES WHEN...

ELSA, WHAT IS THIS?

I DON'T KNOW, LET ME SEE!

UHM...I'VE **NEVER** SEEN IT BEFORE!

JUST THEN, OLINA COMES IN WITH A SNACK AND...

I'VE BROUGHT YOU SOME-- HUH?!? WHERE DID YOU FIND THAT PILLOW?

YOU **KNOW** WHERE IT COMES FROM, OLINA?

I DO! I EMBROIDERED IT MYSELF FOR A LITTLE PRINCESS THAT NOW IS A QUEEN...

Manuscript: Tea Orsi; Layout: Emilio Urbano; Cleanup: Veronica Di Lorenzo and Nicoletta Baldari; Color: Dario Calabria

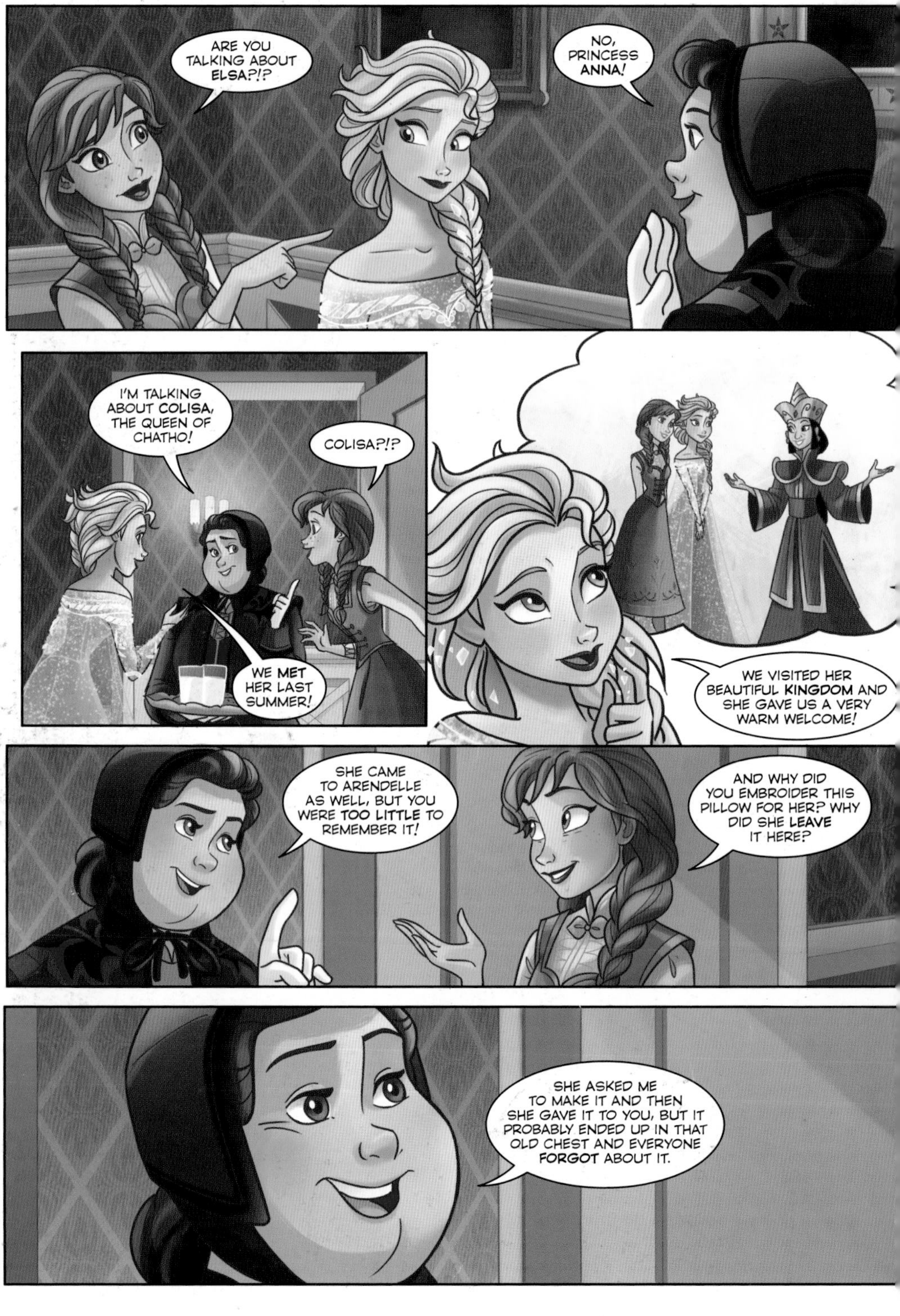
ARE YOU TALKING ABOUT ELSA?!?
NO, PRINCESS ANNA!
I'M TALKING ABOUT COLISA, THE QUEEN OF CHATHO!
COLISA?!?
WE MET HER LAST SUMMER!
WE VISITED HER BEAUTIFUL KINGDOM AND SHE GAVE US A VERY WARM WELCOME!
SHE CAME TO ARENDELLE AS WELL, BUT YOU WERE TOO LITTLE TO REMEMBER IT!
AND WHY DID YOU EMBROIDER THIS PILLOW FOR HER? WHY DID SHE LEAVE IT HERE?
SHE ASKED ME TO MAKE IT AND THEN SHE GAVE IT TO YOU, BUT IT PROBABLY ENDED UP IN THAT OLD CHEST AND EVERYONE FORGOT ABOUT IT.

THIS IS SO MYSTERIOUS! I WANT TO KNOW WHAT THIS SYMBOL MEANS!

YES, WE HAVE TO FIND OUT!

WHY DON'T YOU ASK QUEEN COLISA? I'M SURE SHE'D LOVE TO MEET YOU AGAIN!

GOOD IDEA, OLINA!

THE NEXT MORNING...

I CAN'T WAIT TO BE IN CHATHO!

YES, I HOPE COLISA REMEMBERS ABOUT THE LITTLE PILLOW!

SWOOOSH

197

THE JOURNEY
GOES ON...

THE STORM
WAS SO EXCITING!

YEAH,
KIND OF!

THIS LOOKS
LIKE AN ORCHID!
WE SAW THEM IN
CHATHO!

YOU'RE RIGHT,
BUT I WONDER ABOUT
THE OTHER SYMBOL,
THE SNOWFLAKE...

AND FINALLY...

PRINCESS ANNA,
QUEEN ELSA! IT'S SUCH
A PLEASURE TO SEE
YOU AGAIN!

WE ARE
REALLY HAPPY TOO,
QUEEN COLISA!

WE WANTED TO SHOW YOU THIS! OLINA TOLD US THAT IT WAS A GIFT FROM YOU!

OH DEAR! I REMEMBER IT WELL!

WHAT DOES THIS SYMBOL **MEAN**? WHY DID YOU LEAVE IT TO US?

ANNA!

OH, DON'T WORRY! THAT PILLOW JUST REMINDED ME OF A LOVELY DAY!

I WAS VISITING ARENDELLE WITH MY FAMILY AND YOU WERE STILL VERY LITTLE...

"I ASKED OLINA TO EMBROIDER AN ORCHID ON A LITTLE PILLOW FOR ME, BUT I WANTED LITTLE ELSA TO ADD SOMETHING TOO, SO THAT I COULD HAVE A MEMORY OF HER..."

TELL ME THE **NAME** OF SOMETHING YOU LIKE!

HMMM...

SNOWFLAKE!

"I DESCRIBED TO OLINA THE SYMBOL I HAD IN MIND: A SNOWFLAKE INSIDE AN ORCHID FLOWER AND NEXT DAY JUST BEFORE MY DEPARTURE, THE PILLOW WAS READY..."

DO YOU LIKE IT?

IT'S BEAUTIFUL!

"BUT AT THAT SAME MOMENT LITTLE ANNA STARTED CRYING. OLINA TOLD ME THAT SHE HAD BEEN FEELING A BIT POORLY THAT MORNING..."

NGEEEE NGEEEE!

OH, CALM DOWN LITTLE ONE!

POOR ANNA!

"I WANTED TO DO SOMETHING TO MAKE HER FEEL BETTER. THEN I HAD AN IDEA..."

MAYBE IF SHE CUDDLES MY PILLOW, SHE'LL FEEL ELSA AND ME CLOSER AND SHE'LL CALM DOWN...

"I GAVE IT TO HER AND...IT WORKED! SO I DECIDED THAT SHE NEEDED THAT LOVELY GIFT MORE THAN ME!"

THE MYSTERY IS FINALLY UNVEILED, AND...

THANK YOU. FROM NOW ON I WILL ALWAYS SLEEP WITH MY LITTLE PLUSH PILLOW!

I JUST WONDER WHY OLINA DIDN'T TELL YOU THE STORY HERSELF...

SHE PROBABLY WANTED US TO MAKE AN AMAZING JOURNEY TO MEET YOU AGAIN!

AND IT WAS DEFINETELY WORTH IT!

The End

MEMORIES ON A QUILT

Manuscript: Tea Orsi; Layout: Nicoletta Baldari; Cleanup: Rosa La Barbera; Color: Dario Calabria

THE TWO SISTERS AND OLAF START WORKING...

AND, AFTER A NIGHT SPENT SEWING...

The End

THE ICY RECORD

Manuscript: Tea Orsi; Layout: Benedetta Barone; Cleanup: Marino Gentile; Ink: MichelAngela World; Color: MichelAngela World

BUT KRISTOFF AND ANNA ARE REALLY DETERMINED.

>PANT! PANT!< I WONDER WHY THE HARVESTERS WHO STARTED THE CONTEST YEARS AGO DECIDED TO USE SUCH HEAVY BLOCKS!

AND AFTER SOME HARD WORK...

RECORD

WOW! IF YOU ADD ONE MORE BLOCK THE RECORD WILL BE BROKEN!

WHAT ARE WE WAITING FOR THEN?!

HUH?!

>GASP!<

SWISSSSS

CRAAAAASH

OH, NO!

I TOLD YOU: FORGET IT.

WE CAN'T GIVE UP! LET'S TRY AGAIN.

RECORD

I TRIED MANY, MANY TIMES, BUT IT'S IMPOSSIBLE TO STACK MORE ICE BLOCKS OF THAT SIZE.

WHEN YOU ADD ONE MORE BLOCK, THE STACK STARTS SWAYING AND IT COLLAPSES. THAT'S WHY THE RECORD IS UNTOUCHED!

HMMM... RULES SAY THAT THE BLOCKS MUST BE THAT **WEIGHT**, BUT NOT NECESSARILY THAT SHAPE. CORRECT?

WELL... YES... WHAT DO YOU HAVE IN MIND?

WE'LL **CARVE** THE BLOCKS OURSELVES, AND... PSST PSST...

GOOD IDEA!

205

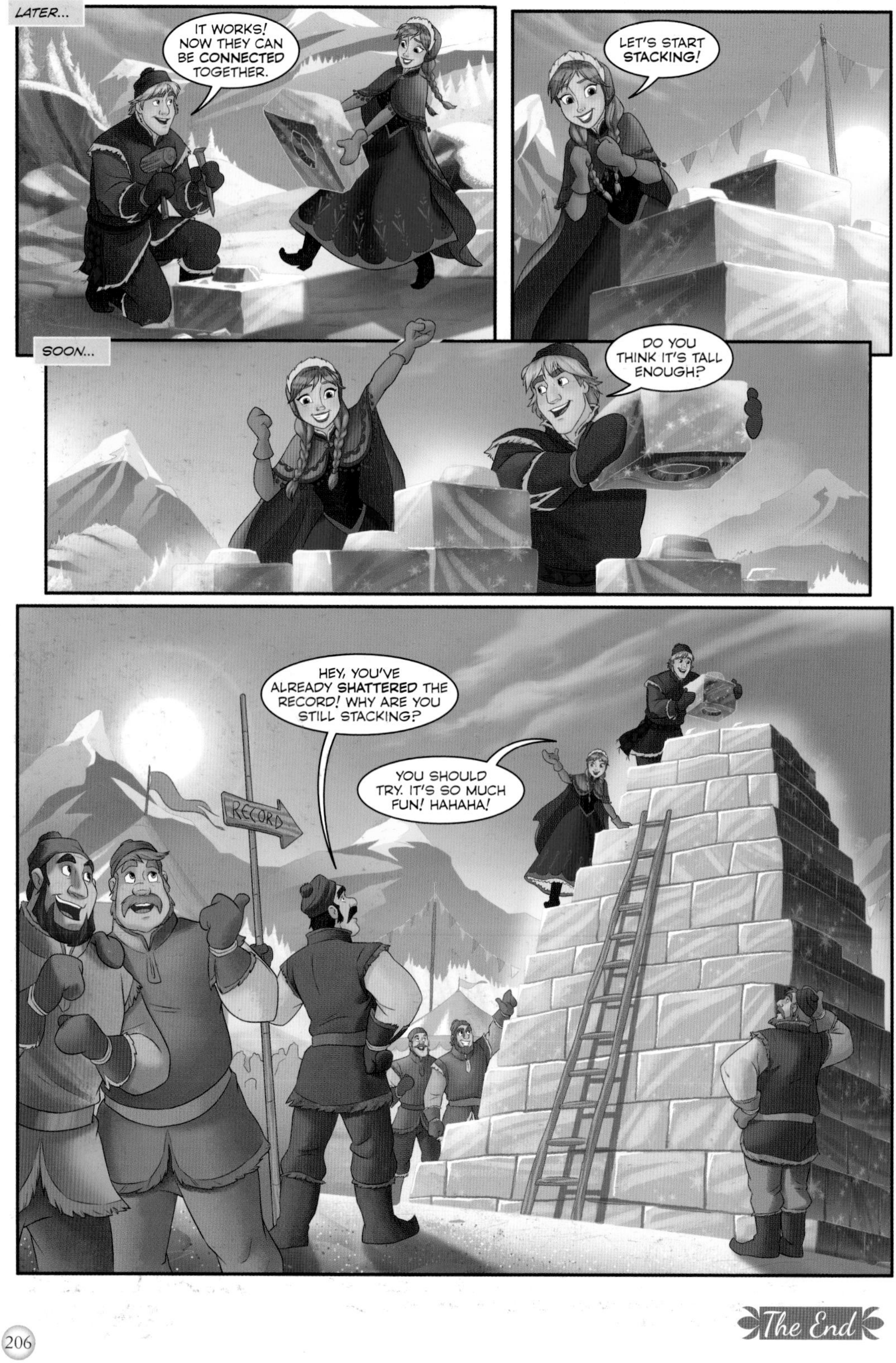
LATER...
IT WORKS! NOW THEY CAN BE CONNECTED TOGETHER.
LET'S START STACKING!
SOON...
DO YOU THINK IT'S TALL ENOUGH?
HEY, YOU'VE ALREADY SHATTERED THE RECORD! WHY ARE YOU STILL STACKING?
YOU SHOULD TRY. IT'S SO MUCH FUN! HAHAHA!
RECORD
The End

A New Hairstyle

Manuscript: Alessandro Ferrari; Layout: Elisabetta Melaranci; Cleanup: Arianna Rea, Federica Salfo; Ink: Michela Frare, Cristina Stella; Color: Dario Calabria

The End

WANDERING SALE

Manuscript: Tea Orsi; Layout: Alberto Zanon; Cleanup: Nicoletta Baldari; Color: Maria Claudia Di Genova

THE STRANGEST CONTEST

IT'S TIME FOR ARENDELLE'S SUMMER PIE-EATING CONTEST!

HOO-HOO! ARE YOU READY TO EAT DELICIOUS LINGONBERRY PIES?

READY... SET... GO!

?!

CHOMP!

CHOMP!

CHOMP!

CHOMP!

CHOMP!

CHOMP!

Original Story By Erica David; Adapted by Chantal Pericoli; Layout: Gianluca Barone; Clean: Marino Gentile; Color: MichelAngela World

WOW! THEY EAT SO... GRACEFULLY! SO... SLOWLY!

THIS IS THE STRANGEST PIE-EATING CONTEST I'VE EVER SEEN!

THAT'S BECAUSE THIS TIME THE RULES ARE DIFFERENT, JA?

I THINK I UNDERSTAND. IT'S NOT ABOUT HOW FAST YOU CAN EAT A PIE, IT'S ABOUT HOW SLOW!

CORRECT! THE SLOWEST CONTESTANT WINS.

THAT DOESN'T SOUND SO HARD...

IT'S TOUGHER THAN YOU THINK. MY PIES ARE SO TASTY, EVERYONE IS IN A HURRY TO GOBBLE THEM UP...

... BUT ONLY THOSE WHO TAKE THEIR TIME WILL TRULY EXPERIENCE THEIR DELICIOUSNESS.

OAKEN, YOU'RE A GENIUS!

SO WHEN DOES THE CONTEST END?

WHEN THE LAST PERSON HAS TAKEN THE LAST BITE.

BUT... THIS COULD LAST ALL NIGHT!

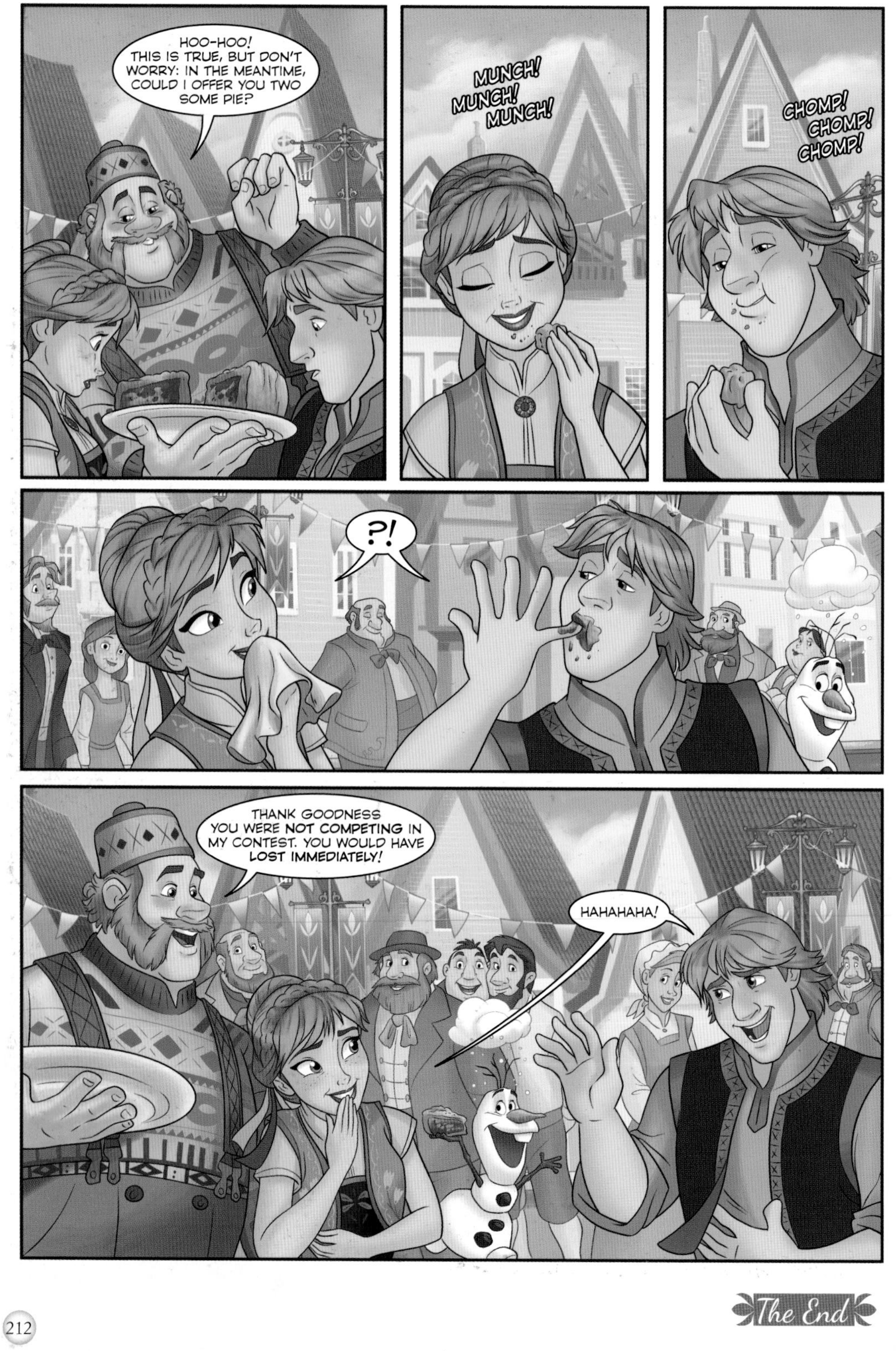
HOO-HOO! THIS IS TRUE, BUT DON'T WORRY: IN THE MEANTIME, COULD I OFFER YOU TWO SOME PIE?
MUNCH! MUNCH! MUNCH!
CHOMP! CHOMP! CHOMP!
?!
THANK GOODNESS YOU WERE **NOT COMPETING** IN MY CONTEST. YOU WOULD HAVE **LOST IMMEDIATELY**!
HAHAHAHA!

The End

THE ZARIAN SEEDS

Part 1

ELSA AND ANNA ARE VISITING THE KINGDOM OF ZARIA WITH SOME OTHER GUESTS...

IT'S SO NICE TO HOST YOU ALL IN SPRING, THE BEST TIME OF THE YEAR!

THE GARDENS ARE IN FULL BLOOM!

THANK YOU FOR INVITING US, KING STEBOR AND QUEEN RENALIA!

YOUR FLOWERS ARE SPECIAL!

THEY CERTAINLY ARE! WOULD YOU BE INTERESTED IN TRADING THESE RARE FLOWERS?

I'M AFRAID THAT MOST OF THEM WOULDN'T GROW IN DIFFERENT CLIMATES, DUKE.

ARE YOU GETTING INTO THE FLOWER BUSINESS, DUKE?

NOT YET, BUT I'D REALLY LIKE TO, QUEEN ELSA!

Manuscript: Tea Orsi; Layout: Emilio Urbano; Cleanup: Manuela Razzi; Color: MichelAngelaworld

THEN, WE MIGHT HAVE GOOD NEWS FOR THE DUKE AND FOR ALL OF YOU!

REGARDING THE FLOWER BUSINESS?

NOW I'M CURIOUS!

TONIGHT WE'LL REVEAL OUR PLAN TO EVERYONE!

IN FACT, AFTER DINNER...

DEAR GUESTS, QUEEN RENALIA AND I WOULD LIKE TO SHARE SOME VERY IMPORTANT NEWS WITH YOU...

I BET THIS IS "THE PLAN"!

AFTER MUCH RESEARCH AND EXPERIMENTATION, OUR GARDENERS HAVE SUCCESSFULLY COMBINED THE SEEDS OF SOME OF OUR RARE PLANTS...

...TO PRODUCE A NEW FLOWER WITH EXTRAORDINARY HEALING PROPERTIES.

AND FINALLY, WE ARE THRILLED TO SHOW THEIR CREATION TO YOU.

PLEASE, BRING THE FLOWER IN!

AND...

SWISH

HERE IT IS! WE ARE STILL LOOKING FOR THE **RIGHT NAME** FOR IT.

IT'S BEAUTIFUL!

WHAT ARE ITS PROPERTIES EXACTLY?

TELL US, PLEASE!

ITS **PETALS** CAN BE MADE INTO A TEA TO ALLEVIATE THE SYMPTOMS OF COLDS, AND ITS LEAVES CAN BE USED TO MAKE A POWERFUL BALM FOR **TOOTHACHE** AND OTHER PAINS.

OAKEN'S GOING TO LOVE THIS!

INDEED! WHICH IS WHY WE WANTED TO SHARE IT WITH YOU!

REALLY?!? THAT'S EXCELLENT NEWS!

WE WANT TO GIVE YOU SEEDS SO YOU CAN **PLANT** THEM IN YOUR KINGDOMS!

THE GARDENERS BELIEVE THAT THE FLOWER IS LIKELY TO SPROUT IN DIFFERENT CLIMATES, TOO.

BUT IT NEEDS **SPECIAL CARE** THAT WE'LL TELL YOU ABOUT LATER.

FIRST I WILL DISTRIBUTE THE...

GASP! **WHERE ARE THE** SEEDS?

HUH?!? HOPEFULLY THEY JUST FORGOT TO PUT THEM ON THE TROLLEY...

BUT, WHEN THE KING SUMMONS ONE OF THE GARDENERS...

I'M SORRY, BUT THE VASE WITH THE SEEDS IS **NOWHERE** TO BE FOUND!

HOW IS THAT POSSIBLE?

KING STEBOR NEEDS **EVERYBODY'S** HELP!

216

ELSA AND I THINK WE SHOULD ALL TRY SEARCHING FOR THE SEEDS...

THIS IS VERY KIND OF YOU, BUT THE GARDENERS WILL TAKE CARE OF THIS.

IT'S TOO DARK NOW. WE'LL START THE INVESTIGATIONS TOMORROW.

AS YOU PREFER, KING STEBOR!

THOSE SEEDS COULDN'T HAVE VANISHED!

THEY HAVE TO BE HERE SOMEWHERE!

WHAT A WASTE OF OUR TIME!

OOPS! DID I JUST SAY THAT OUT LOUD?

?!?

ANYWAY... I WON'T WAIT UNTIL TOMORROW!

WHERE IS HE GOING?

I'M SO SORRY...

WHAT IF THE WIND BLEW THEM AWAY?

NO ONE NOTICED THAT THE DUKE WALKED AWAY...

WELL, HE MUMBLED HE WAS GOING TO SEARCH FOR THE SEEDS.

BUT THE KING FORBADE IT!

I KNOW, BUT... I'LL JUST CHECK IF HE NEEDS HELP! IT'S VERY DARK OUTSIDE!

ANNA! WAIT! YOU WILL GET IN TROUBLE!

End of Part 1

THE ZARIAN SEEDS

Part 2

ELSA CAN'T HELP BUT FOLLOW ANNA TO THE ROYAL GARDENS, AND...

ANNA, DID YOU FIND SOMETHING?

I THINK I WAS RIGHT...

LOOK!

THE DUKE IS TALKING TO ONE OF THE GARDENERS!

ARE YOU SURE YOU DID NOT SEE ANYONE ENTERING THE GARDEN?

YES, SIR! ONLY THE ROYAL GARDENERS HAVE ADMITTANCE THERE.

TALKING?! THAT IS AN INTERROGATORY!

THEN, MAYBE SOME GARDENER STOLE THE HEALING SEEDS TO SELL THEM! MAYBE... YOU?

N-NO, I WOULD NEVER DO THAT!

Manuscript: Tea Orsi; Layout: Emilio Urbano; Cleanup: Manuela Razzi; Color: MichelAngelaworld

GRRR! THIS SITUATION IS RIDICULOUS!

I GUESS HE DIDN'T FIND ANY CLUE.

I CAN'T UNDERSTAND WHY HE'S SO EAGER TO FIND THE SEEDS BEFORE EVERYONE ELSE...

UNLESS HE WANTS TO BE THE ONLY ONE TO POSSESS THEM!

YES... SOMETIMES HE IS A BIT OBSESSED WITH RICHNESS. AND THAT HEALING FLOWER COULD MAKE ANYONE VERY RICH!

WE'D BETTER GO IN NOW OR THE OTHERS WILL START SUSPECTING US INSTEAD!

BUT... I WANT TO KEEP SEARCHING!

IF THE DUKE OF WESELTON REALLY WANTS TO FIND THE SEEDS FOR HIMSELF, WE MUST FIND THEM FIRST.

OKAY, WE CAN TAKE THE OTHER **PATH** TO THE PALACE!

GOOD IDEA. LET'S GO!

I'M COMING!

BUT SOON...

YIKES!

HUH?!?

EXCUSE US, ARE YOU LOOKING FOR SOMETHING?

YOUR MAJESTIES!?! I...

I'M TERRIBLY SORRY, BUT I... I SEEM TO HAVE **LOST** ALL THE SEEDS THAT THE KING WANTED TO GIVE YOU...

LOST?! HOW DID IT HAPPEN?

IT WAS AN ACCIDENT! I WAS CARRYING THE VASE TO THE PALACE...

"WHEN I TRIPPED OVER A ROCK, AND..."

AND NOW... I CAN'T FIND THE SEEDS. IT'S TOO DARK!

DON'T WORRY! WE JUST NEED MORE LANTERNS!

THERE ARE A LOT OF THEM AT THE PALACE. I'M SURE WE CAN GET SOME!

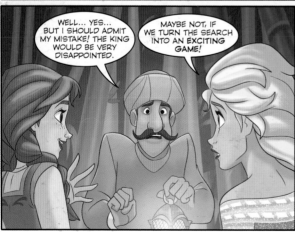

WELL... YES... BUT I SHOULD ADMIT MY MISTAKE! THE KING WOULD BE VERY DISAPPOINTED.

MAYBE NOT, IF WE TURN THE SEARCH INTO AN EXCITING GAME!

I HAVE A PLAN...

SO...

LET'S ALL GO TOGETHER WITH THE LANTERNS. EACH OF US WILL FIND AND COLLECT OUR OWN SEEDS TO TAKE HOME!

WHAT A GREAT IDEA, PRINCESS ANNA!

HOW EXCITING!

WHAT?!!

I WILL NEVER KNEEL TO GET SOME SEEDS!

AS YOU PREFER, DUKE!

SO THE NIGHTTIME SEARCH BEGINS...

YAY! I FOUND ONE!

LET ME GIVE YOU THE INSTRUCTIONS I WAS MENTIONING BEFORE!

PLEASE, REMEMBER TO GATHER SOME ZARIAN SOIL, TOO.

SOIL AMENDMENT WILL HELP THE SEEDS WHEN THEY ARE TRANSPLANTED IN DIFFERENT CLIMATES!

A FEW WEEKS LATER, IN ARENDELLE...

KING STEBOR AND QUEEN RENALIA WERE RIGHT! THEY BLOOMED!

I JUST GOT A LETTER FROM THEM. THEY CALLED THE FLOWERS **ARENDELLE STARS**, BECAUSE WE HELPED FIND THE SEEDS!

I WONDER HOW THE DUKE FEELS ABOUT THAT NAME?

I WONDER IF HIS SEEDS SPROUTED...

"I DOUBT IT, BECAUSE HE DIDN'T LISTEN TO THE ADVICE..."

I CAN'T UNDERSTAND! I ORDERED MY BUTLER TO COLLECT PERFECTLY CLEAN SEEDS!

AND NEXT TIME, PLEASE REMIND ME TO FIND A BETTER WAY TO EXPLOIT ZARIA'S RICHES!

The End

BUZZING MOMENTS

ANNA AND ELSA ARE HAVING A QUIET TIME, WHEN...

OLAF IS FOLLOWING A BEE!

THAT IS ONE OF HIS FAVORITE PASTIMES!

LA LA LA!

BZZZ

WAIT! THERE ARE **TWO** BEES!

DON'T WORRY! THEY **LOVE** HIM!

OH DEAR! LOOK AT HIM!

I TOLD YOU THEY REALLY LIKE HIM, ANNA!

BZZZZZZZZZZZZ

AWWW! WHAT A BIG WARM HUG!

Manuscript: Tea Orsi; Layout: Emilio Urbano; Cleanup: Veronica Di Lorenzo; Color: Dario Calabria

The End

THE CASUAL PLAYER

CAUGHT!

NOW IT'S MY TURN!

SWISH

NOOO! IT'S TOO HIGH!

BONK

SVEN?!? WHAT GREAT CATCH!

YOU SHOULD HAVE TOLD US THAT YOU WANTED TO PLAY TOO!

Manuscript: Tea Orsi; Layout: Emilio Urbano; Cleanup: Letizia Algeri; Color: Dario Calabria

The End

As Tall As A Snowgie

ELSA, ANNA AND OLAF HAVE JUST ARRIVED AT THE ICE PALACE...

MARSHMALLOW LOOKS EXHAUSTED...

YES, THE SNOWGIES SEEM MORE LIVELY THAN USUAL.

POING POING POING POING POING

UHM... I THINK I KNOW THAT GAME THEY ARE PLAYING...

POING

REALLY?

YES! IT'S CALLED "BE AS TALL AS MARSHMALLOW!"

SO THAT'S WHY THEY KEEP JUMPING...

POING

LOOKS LIKE FUN!

I'M COOOMING, LITTLE BROTHERS!

Manuscript: Tea Orsi; Layout and Cleanup: Manuela Razzi; Color: Stefania Santi

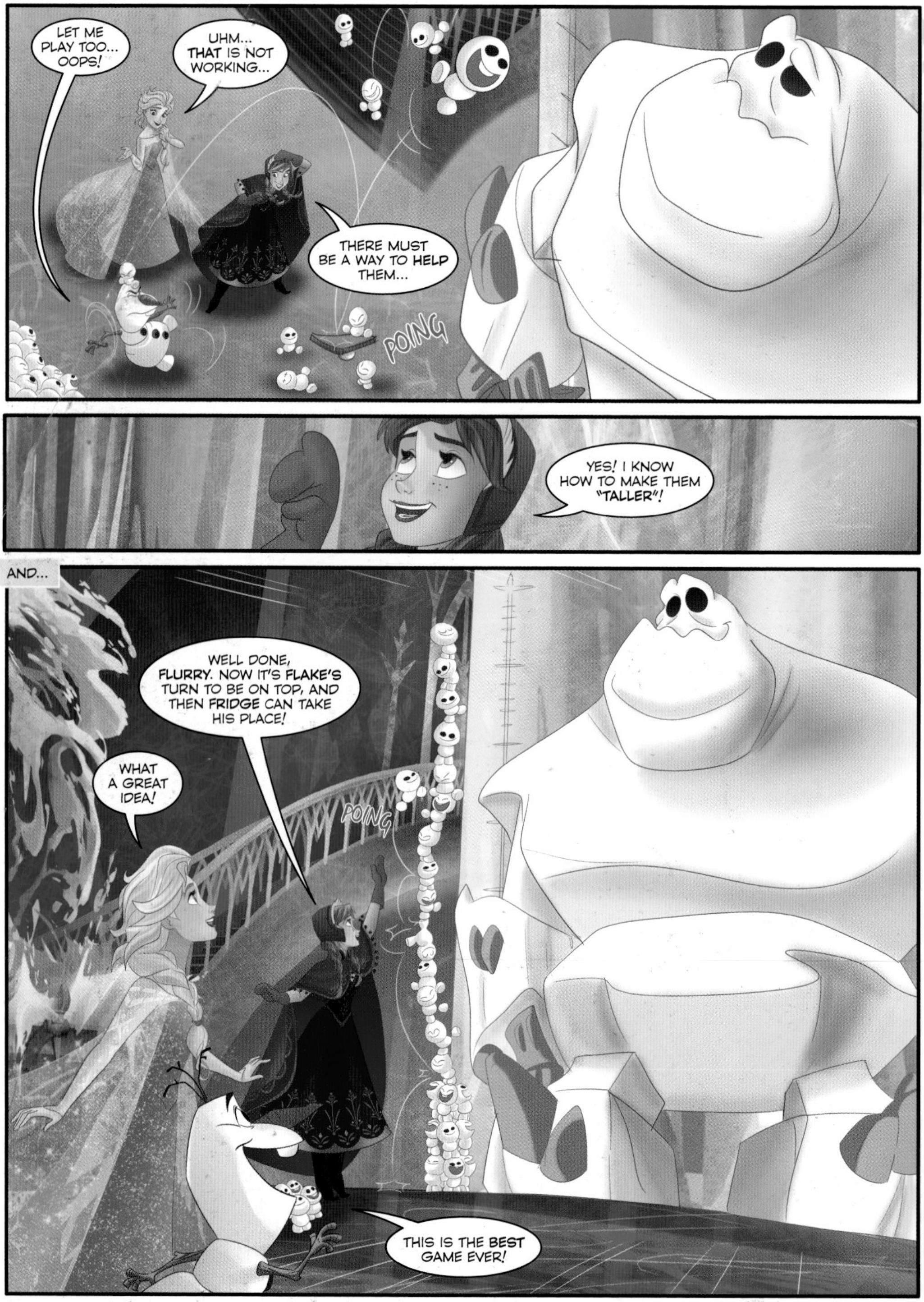
LET ME PLAY TOO... OOPS!
UHM... THAT IS NOT WORKING...
THERE MUST BE A WAY TO HELP THEM...
POING
YES! I KNOW HOW TO MAKE THEM "TALLER"!
AND...
WELL DONE, FLURRY. NOW IT'S FLAKE'S TURN TO BE ON TOP, AND THEN FRIDGE CAN TAKE HIS PLACE!
WHAT A GREAT IDEA!
POING
THIS IS THE BEST GAME EVER!

The End

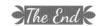

THE KING OF HUGS

Manuscript: Alessandro Ferrari; Layout: Elisabetta Melaranci; Cleanup: Arianna Rea, Federica Salfo; Ink: Michela Frare, Cristina Stella; Color: Dario Calabria

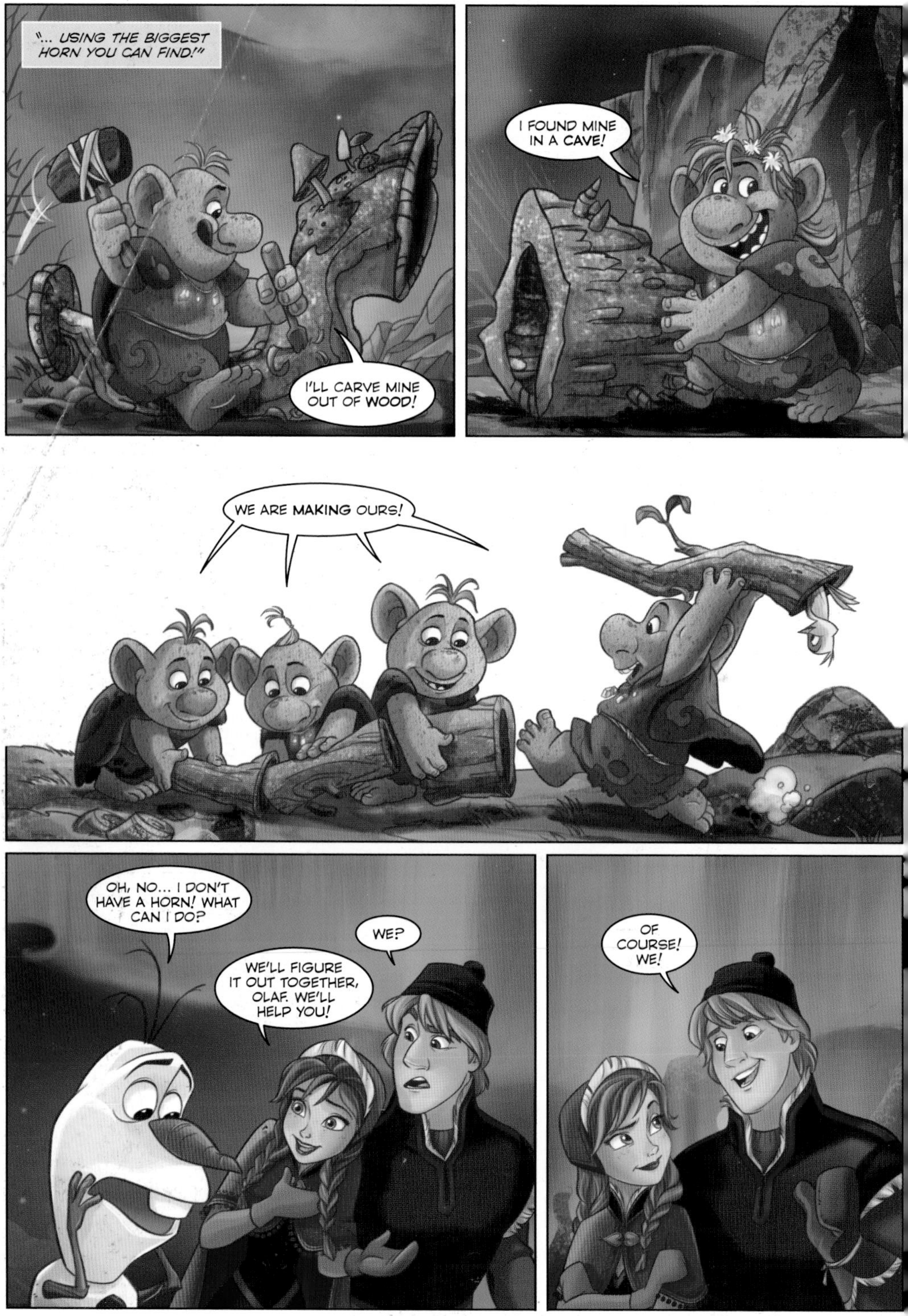
"... USING THE BIGGEST HORN YOU CAN FIND!"
I'LL CARVE MINE OUT OF WOOD!
I FOUND MINE IN A CAVE!
WE ARE MAKING OURS!
OH, NO... I DON'T HAVE A HORN! WHAT CAN I DO?
WE'LL FIGURE IT OUT TOGETHER, OLAF. WE'LL HELP YOU!
WE?
OF COURSE! WE!

SOON IT'S CONTEST DAY!

CCCCc

ALL THE TROLLS ARE REALLY GREAT...

DDDDD D

EEFFFF GGGG AAAA

... SOME OF THEM ARE EXTRAORDINARILY GREAT!

WITH THE HELP OF HIS FRIENDS...

SING AS LOUD AS YOU CAN, OLAF! WE BELIEVE IN YOU!

THANK YOU, THANK YOU, THANK YOU!

... OLAF GETS READY TO BEAT THEM ALL WITH HIS ICE HORN!

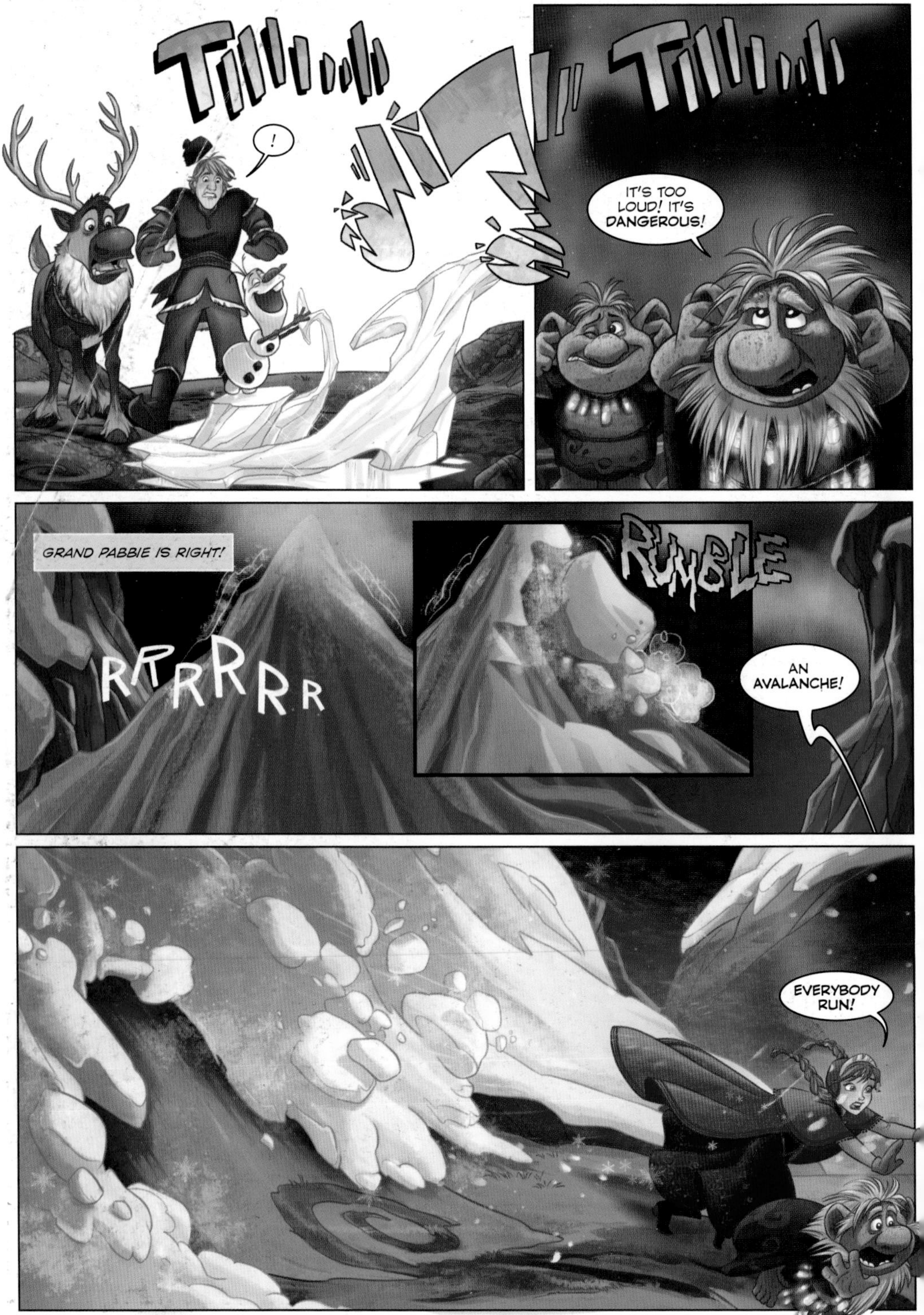

TIIIIII
!
TIIIIIIII
IT'S TOO LOUD! IT'S DANGEROUS!
GRAND PABBIE IS RIGHT!
RRRRRRR
RUMBLE
AN AVALANCHE!
EVERYBODY RUN!

PHEEEEW! THAT WAS CLOSE.

LUCKILY WE ARE ALL SAFE!

?!

OLAF? YOU ARE RIGHT, SVEN! OLAF IS MISSING!

OLAF! WHERE ARE YOU?

HE SHOULD BE THERE SOMEWHERE...

ARE WE REALLY LOOKING FOR A SNOWMAN IN THE SNOW?

!

SNIFF
SNIFF

!

SVEN? WHAT HAPPENED?

OLAF! YOU ARE SAFE!

WOW! I THINK I WON THE CONTEST!

LOOKS LIKE YOU'RE GETTING A YEAR FULL OF HUGS, OLAF! THAT MAKES YOU THE THE KING OF HUGS!

HOORAY!

The End

A Book for Marshmallow

ANNA IS EXCITED ABOUT A BOOK SHE FOUND...

MARSHMALLOW WOULD LOVE THESE PICTURES OF SNOWY LANDSCAPES!

LET'S TAKE THE BOOK TO HIM!

BUT, AT THE ICE PALACE...

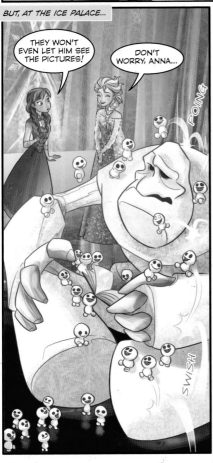

THEY WON'T EVEN LET HIM SEE THE PICTURES!

DON'T WORRY, ANNA...

POING

SWISH

THE SNOWGIES ONLY WANT TO TAKE A LOOK AT THE BOOK WITH HIM...

AND I'M SURE HE'LL ENJOY IT AS MUCH AS THEM!

Manuscript: Tea Orsi; Layout: Alberto Zanon; Cleanup: Miriam Gambino; Color: Dario Calabria

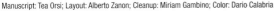

The End

THE SECRET CODE

Manuscript: Tea Orsi; Layout: Nicoletta Baldari; Cleanup: Veronica Di Lorenzo; Color: Alessandra Bracaglia

The End

CREATIVE RIDE

ANNA AND ELSA ARE HEADING HOME AFTER A LONG RIDE...

WOW, YOU'RE FAST!

COME ON, YOU'VE NEARLY REACHED ME!

BUT...

CRACK

YIKES! WHAT'S GOING ON?

GASP!

SHRIEEEEEK

GASP! YOUR WHEEL IS COMPLETELY BROKEN!

I THINK I RODE OVER SOMETHING SHARP...

Manuscript: Tea Orsi; Layout: Manuela Razzi; Clean up: Letizia Algeri; Color: Stefania Santi

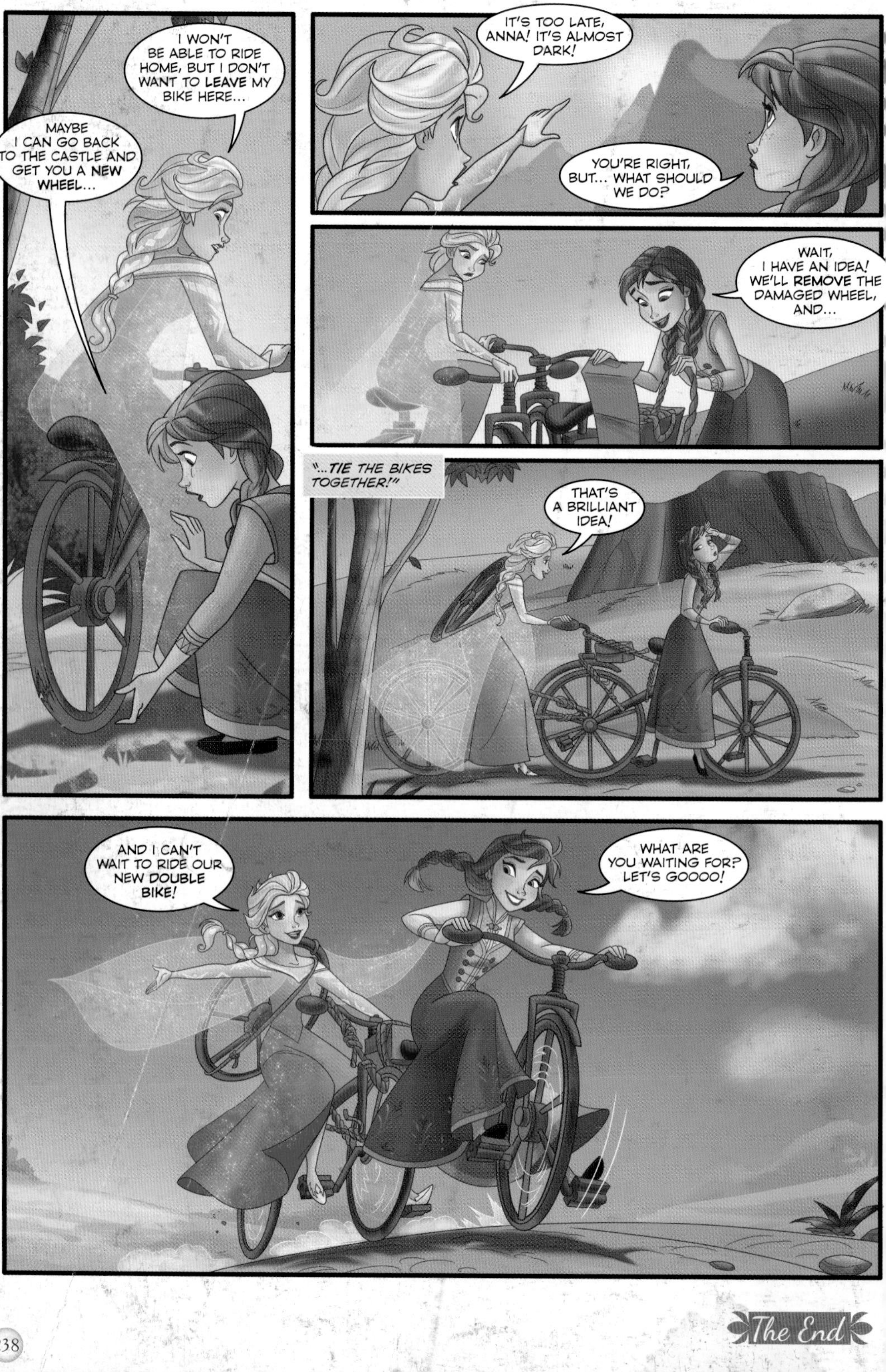
I WON'T BE ABLE TO RIDE HOME, BUT I DON'T WANT TO LEAVE MY BIKE HERE...
MAYBE I CAN GO BACK TO THE CASTLE AND GET YOU A NEW WHEEL...
IT'S TOO LATE, ANNA! IT'S ALMOST DARK!
YOU'RE RIGHT, BUT... WHAT SHOULD WE DO?
WAIT, I HAVE AN IDEA! WE'LL REMOVE THE DAMAGED WHEEL, AND...
"...TIE THE BIKES TOGETHER!"
THAT'S A BRILLIANT IDEA!
AND I CAN'T WAIT TO RIDE OUR NEW DOUBLE BIKE!
WHAT ARE YOU WAITING FOR? LET'S GOOOO!

The End

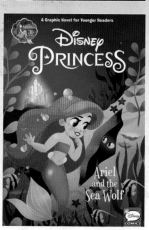

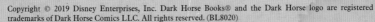

Disney